MEET THE GIRL TAL

Sabrina Wells is petite, with curly auburn hair, sparkling hazel eyes, and a bubbly personality. Sabrina loves magazines, shopping, sleepovers, and most of all, she loves talking to her best friends.

Katie Campbell's a straight-A student and super athlete. With her blond hair, blue eyes, and matching clothes, she's everyone's idea of little miss perfect. But Katie has a few surprises for everyone, including herself!

Randy Zak has just moved to Acorn Falls from New York City, and is she ever cool! With her 'radical' spiked haircut and her hip New York clothes, Randy teaches everyone just how much fun it is to be different.

Allison Cloud is a Native American Indian. Allison's super smart and really beautiful. But she has one major problem: She's thirteen years old, five foot seven, and still growing!

Here's what they're talking about in
Girl Talk

SABRINA: That new guy on the hockey team is really cute. And I love his French accent!

KATIE: Yeah, and he's an incredible hockey player, too. Last year he was Most Valuable Player for his team.

SABRINA: Hmmm, I wonder if he had a girlfriend back in his old home town.

KATIE: Sabrina, I think you have a crush on him!

SABRINA: I think you do, too!

MIXED FEELINGS

By L. E. Blair

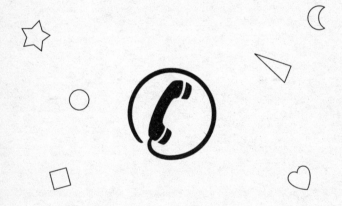

GIRL TALK® series created by Western Publishing Company, Inc.

Produced by Angel Entertainment, Inc.

Western Publishing Company, Inc., Racine, Wisconsin 53404

Text by Cathy Lasry

Chapter One

"It's hard to believe you were ever a flag girl, Katie Campbell," I said to my reflection in the mirror. I was standing in the dimly lit visitors' locker room of Bradley Junior High's ice hockey team. Since I'm the only girl on the team, I change in the visitors' locker room during regular practice. When there's a game, I change upstairs in one of the girls' bathrooms, but it's a pain. I've only been on the team a few months, but it feels like years since I quit the flag squad and joined the ice hockey team.

I pulled my practice jersey over my white undershirt, then I quickly brushed and braided my hair. I always wear my hair in a French braid under my helmet. I tucked my braid under my jersey. I don't like to give anybody anything to pull out there on the ice. Hockey can get pretty rough sometimes.

I looked at my reflection again and smiled.

It was hard to tell I was a girl because of all the hockey padding I was wearing.

As soon as I finished dressing, I sat down on the bench and reached for my skates. Suddenly I heard whispering behind me. I quickly looked around, but I didn't see anyone. Then someone giggled.

The visitors' locker room shares a wall with the home-team locker room. I looked around and noticed that one of the knots in the wall had mysteriously disappeared, leaving a definite hole. Someone giggled again. I picked up my water bottle and walked over to the row of sinks. Calmly I filled the bottle and whispered, "I'm going to get you guys."

I turned around and made as if I were going to walk back toward my skates. Instead, I sprinted for the wall and squirted the water right into the hole.

"Aaargh!" someone screamed from the other side of the wall.

I giggled, ran over, and picked up my skates and my stick. Just then I heard Coach Budd's whistle, so I jogged out onto the rink in my socks. I was the first one on the bench. Jamming my helmet on my head and dropping my heavy hockey skates onto the floor, I sighed. I was getting so tired of wearing these old, scratched brown skates. I had borrowed them from my best friend, Sabrina Wells. Actually, I had borrowed them from her older brother Mark, who is in the eight grade and had already outgrown them. I really need new ones, but they're very expensive. I know the exact skates I want. Every time I go shopping, I walk into my favorite sporting goods store and look at them. My birthday is less than two weeks away, and I keep hoping I'll get them for a present. I've already told my mom that they're the only thing I really want. She keeps saying that what I really *need* is a new bed-spread. A bedspread for my birthday? I hope she's joking.

Anyway, the guys had started to troop out of the locker room by the time I had my skates laced. I think it's funny that guys always complain that girls take so long to get ready. I'm always the first one on the bench at every practice.

"Nice shot!" Flip Walsh said, slapping me on the back. He hit kind of hard and I almost fell off the bench. Sometimes the guys forget

I'm a girl. I have to admit that we all look alike in our helmets, uniforms, skates, and mounds of padding.

"That was really funny!" Brian Williams exclaimed, plopping down next to me on the bench. "I was totally crying."

"Very funny," Scottie Silver echoed sarcastically, sitting down next to Brian. I looked over at him, then toward Coach Budd coming across the ice, then back at Scottie. I giggled. Scottie's hair was all wet!

"Get caught in the rain, Silver?" Jeff Atkins asked, laughing.

"Or did you decide to take a pre-practice shower?" Flip wanted to know.

"Ha, ha," Scottie muttered, and then turned toward me. "I'm going to get you for this, K.C." The guys on the team call me K.C. Now even the coach uses the nickname. Scottie is the team captain, and he decided that the name Katie was just too feminine to shout out over the ice.

I gave Scottie an *I don't know what you're talking about* look just as the coach came up to the bench. And besides, *I* hadn't been the one trying to peek into their locker room, so it served Scottie right.

As the coach started talking, I thought back to the way the guys had treated me during team tryouts at the beginning of the season. They had been really rough on the ice and had tried to scare me away from joining the team. Coach Budd had even backed them up. At the time, it hadn't made sense because I got along with most of them when I was a flag girl. I guess I threatened their masculinity or something by being a good hockey player. But I proved that I could handle it, and now I'm actually in the starting lineup for the left-wing position.

"What's he talking about?" Peter Mullins, our goalie, asked in a whisper, dragging me back to the present.

"Huh?" I replied.

"It's near the end of the season," Peter went on as if he hadn't heard me. "How can we get a new player?"

A new player? What was going on, I wondered.

Just then a dark-haired boy I'd never seen before approached the bench. "Who's that?" Scottie asked.

"Guys," the coach began, "this is Michel

Beauvais. He just moved here from Canada. He was MVP during the championships up there last year. I'm really glad to have him with us."

Someone giggled. I heard someone say, "Michel?" but I couldn't tell who it was.

"Michel is French for Michael," Coach Budd continued firmly. "And I know all of you will join me in welcoming him to Acorn falls and Bradley Junior High." The coach paused for a long moment. No one said anything. So the coach added a stern, "Right?"

A low chorus of *yeah's* came from the bench, but that was about it. I took a moment to study the new player. Michel was tall with black hair cut fairly short and really dark eyes. My friend Sabrina was going to go wild when she saw him. Sabrina's favorite thing — besides reading her horoscope, teen magazines, and being on a diet — is boys.

Michel just stood there, staring at all of us as if he was daring anyone to say anything about his name again. Suddenly it occurred to me that maybe he only spoke French and hadn't understood what we were talking about.

"Doesn't he have to try out?" Flip asked in astonishment.

Coach Budd looked at Flip and narrowed his eyes. "It's very late in the season, and I think Michel's record speaks for itself," Coach Budd responded.

I was kind of surprised at that. I mean, we had all gone through a killer week of tryouts at the beginning of the season. I had had to take a bath every night because my muscles were so sore. It wasn't fair that this guy got to skip all of that — even if he was an MVP last season.

"All right, team!" Coach Budd called, blowing his whistle. I think he wanted to change the subject. "We've got a big game coming up this weekend. If we beat the Minneapolis Mongols, we'll be on our way to the state championships. Michel is going to be a valuable addition to our squad." He paused and eyed each of us individually. Then he blew his whistle again. "Let's get on the ice and warm up."

We began skating in circles around the rink, with our hockey sticks. We do this to warm up our muscles so we don't pull anything. The coach is always telling us that a good warm-up is essential. I believe him.

Michel skated the whole warm-up by himself. No one went near him. I felt kind of bad for him, since that was exactly how the guys had treated me when I first tried out. But I was still a little mad that Mr. MVP Michel didn't even have to try out, so I left him alone, too.

I know it's not easy to move to a new place, though. One of my best friends, Randy Zak, moved here at the beginning of the year from New York City, after her parents got divorced. She really hated it at first — she missed the city and her friends and her father. It must be even worse to start in the middle of a school year, not to mention the middle of hockey season.

Coach Budd blew his whistle once again. Then he divided us into three teams. My team sat out first while the other two teams scrimmaged.

Michel played left defense. Even though no one would pass him the puck, I could see why he had been the MVP last season. He covered his area like a professional. Nothing, and nobody, got by him.

Scottie, playing on the other team, sent a shot toward Brian. Brian was behind Michel and he didn't have a prayer of seeing that puck. Michel snatched it and started across the center line. Flip poked at the puck and tried to check Michel. Michel looked around as if to see if anyone was open. Not one of his teammates was making any effort to help him out. Michel sent a shot to the right and then drove around Flip to the left. From thirty feet out, Michel took a slap shot that nailed the net over Peter's right shoulder. The goalie didn't even get to use his stick. Michel's shot was that fast.

Silence fell over the rink. This guy was good! I don't think any of us really expected him to be good. Michel calmly skated across the ice as if he made shots like that every day. Maybe he did.

Even though I thought Michel was stuck up, it was funny to see Scottie's shocked expression. Captain Scottie Silver was clearly no longer the best player on the team — and he knew it.

After fifteen minutes, Scottie's team sat down and mine went in. Having watched Michel completely shut down the left side of the ice, my team decided to concentrate on Michel's right side — which was our left side. It meant that, at left wing, I was getting the puck a lot.

"K.C.!" Brett Hall shouted from behind our

goalie. He sent the puck flying toward me. It hit my stick with a loud thunk, and I was off. Getting around the defense, I looked for an open man to pass to. Before I even looked around, Michel was on me. I flicked a short pass in the air to Eamon Daniels, my center. He faked the goalie to the right and popped the puck into the left-hand corner. Goal!

"All right!" Brett shouted, skating toward me. He patted my helmet with his gloved hand. "Nice pass, K. C.!"

"Good going, guys!" Coach Budd called out. "Let's switch teams again."

Michel's team went to the bench, and Scottie's came out onto the ice. It was obvious that Scottie felt as if he had something to prove. He was playing with a vengeance.

We finished the scrimmage, bruised and tired, and then the coach told us to hurry up and change and report back for a meeting.

I stomped over to the visitors' locker room and took off my heavy old skates and two pairs of sweaty socks. It felt good to wiggle my toes again. I showered and changed and was back on the bench before any of the other guys.

"Katie!" someone called from the bleachers.

I turned and saw my friend Sabrina waving at me. We had plans to go to her house after my practice. I love going to Sabs's house. Her house is usually like one big party, with so many kids around all the time. She has four older brothers, including a twin brother, Sam. It's so different from my house where it's just my mother, my sister Emily and me.

I waved back at Sabs and then sat down to wait for the rest of the team. Michel was the first one out of the locker room. He walked over to the bench and looked at me hesitantly.

"Hi," I said to him. If he was going to be on the team, I would try to be friends with him. It wasn't his fault he had missed our killer try-outs. Anyways, he'd probably gone through tryouts at his own school.Before I could open my mouth to set him straight, Scottie, and Flip joined us on the bench.

"You're a great player," Flip commented. "You Canadians must breathe hockey."

"Really," Scottie added. "That was some goal shot."

Michel nodded his thanks. So the guys had decided to make peace with our new team mate. I knew it must have been hard for Scottie to compliment Michel. It seems as if it's not very easy for boys to admit when another guy is better than they are.

"Don't you think so?" Flip asked, turning toward me.

"Oh, you watched the practice?" Michel asked. "It's nice that Coach Budd allows spectators. It gives us somebody to show off in front of." He looked at me and grinned, his dark eyes crinkling at the corners.

Flip and Scottie started laughing. Michel looked questioningly at them, obviously confused. His eyes narrowed slightly, probably because he thought they were making fun of him in some way.

"K.C. had a great seat," Flip said, sputtering with laughter. "She was the speedy little left winger during the second scrimmage."

Michel's mouth dropped open in shock. I started to giggle, he looked so surprised.

"You're K.C.?' he asked in astonishment.

"Yup," Scottie answered for me, obviously enjoying Michel's shock. "She starts for us, and she has the second-highest number of goals this season. Right behind me."

In a moment, I thought Michel's chin was

going to hit the floor. "But you are a girl," he said finally. "K.C. is a boy's name."

"It stands for Katie Campbell," I replied, trying to keep my voice even. I had been through this at the beginning of the season, so I should be used to it by now. But it makes me so mad when people act shocked that a girl can play hockey as well as a boy.

"Oh," Michel began, as the rest of the team straggled out to the bench. He was about to open his mouth to say something else when the coach's whistle cut him off.

I tried to pay attention as Coach Budd discussed strategy for beating the Mongols. My mind kept wandering, though. I hoped I wasn't going to have to prove myself as a hockey player again because of Michel. But if Scottie Silver and the other guys could make the effort to be friends with Michel, then so would I. At least for the good of the team.

Chapter Two

"Oh, my gosh, Katie!" Sabs exclaimed as we walked down the street toward her house. "That new guy is *so* cute! And that French accent!"

I zipped up my ski jacket without answering her. There was a definite bite in the air.

"Don't you think so, Katie?" Sabs asked, ignoring my silence. "You are so lucky to be on the hockey team with him. You get to see him every day!"

"Great," I muttered under my breath. Just what I needed. Another guy on the hockey team ready to give me a hard time.

"You are so lucky!" Sabs repeated.

"Do we have to keep talking about him?" I asked when Sabs had paused for breath.

"K. C.!" I recognized Michel's voice calling from behind us.

I kept walking, pretending that I didn't

hear. "Oh, look! It's him!" Sabs exclaimed, grabbing my arm. "Katie, wait a minute!"

I turned around and saw Michel jogging up to us, lugging his equipment bag with him. I took a deep breath. We are on the same team, I reminded myself. "Welcome to the team," I began. "You're a great player." That was no lie, at least.

"*Merci*," Michel answered. "I'm very happy that I didn't have to miss out on any hockey this season."

The wind suddenly blew up, and I pulled my scarf up over my chin. It was getting really cold out.

"Hi, I'm Sabrina," Sabs cut in, sticking her red-mittened hand in front of Michel's face.

He grinned and shook her hand. "*Bonjour*, Sabrina. It is very nice to meet you."

"You, too," she replied and blushed.

"Do you go to Bradley Junior High School, also?" Michel asked Sabs, shifting his hockey bag on his shoulder.

"We're in the seventh grade together," I replied for Sabs.

"*Bien*," Michel replied. "I'm in the seventh class as well. Maybe we'll have some classes together."

"That would be great!" Sabs practically gushed. "You're going to love it here."

"I certainly hope so," Michel answered, his dark eyes crinkling at the corners as he smiled. I have to admit he did look really cute when he smiled like that. "Ah, here is my street," he said, pointing down Maple Street.

"Really?" Sabs asked, sounding excited. "That's where our friend Randy lives." She pointed at the big converted barn on the corner of Maple and Main Street where Randy lives with her mother.

"So, I will meet my neighbors?" Michel asked, stopping on the corner.

"Definitely," Sabs said firmly. "And I'll introduce you to everyone at school."

"*Très bien. Merci,*" he answered, starting off down the block. "I will see you at school tomorrow." He turned toward me. "K. C., you are a good hockey player. That was a very nice assist. *Au revoir.*" And with that, he was gone.

Sabs talked all the way to her house about how wonderful Michel was. I had to admit that I was beginning to like him, too. It was a relief to realize that I might not have to prove myself all over again to a new teammate.

When we got to Sabs's house, she opened the back door and we ran smack into Randy and Allison.

"What are you guys doing here?" I asked in confusion. Sabs hadn't mentioned they were coming over, too.

Randy shrugged and shot Sabs a look. I turned to stare at Sabs. She was raising and lowering her eyebrows really fast and opening her eyes very wide.

"What's wrong with you, Sabs?" I asked directly.

"Uh . . . nothing . . . um . . ." Sabs mumbled. "I . . . uh . . ."

"We . . .ah . . ." Allison stuttered, cutting Sabs off. Allison's brown eyes were opened wide in surprise, and she kept smoothing an imaginary wrinkle out of her yellow skirt.

"What's wrong with you guys?" I asked, beginning to get a little suspicious. Something was definitely up.

"How was practice?" Randy said, cutting in, and pushing up the sleeves of her long-sleeved black T-shirt. Randy is a really wild dresser — I guess that's because she's from New York. She had on this long dark purple knit jumper over her T-shirt.

"Hey, you guys!" Sabs exclaimed, dropping her coat among the others hanging on the row of hooks next to the back door. Then she sat down and started pulling off her boots. "There's this new guy on the hockey team. His name is Michel Beauvais. He's from Canada, and he's got this great French accent. He's in the seventh grade with us. And talk about cute! Black hair, beautiful brown eyes, and his smile is to die for, practically. Anyway ... I wonder what sign he is. We may be very compatible."

"Isn't it kind of late in the season for a new player?" Allison asked, flipping her long black hair over her shoulder.

"Yeah," I said with a sigh. "And he didn't have to try out or anything. Basically, it's not very fair, but Coach Budd says he was MVP for his team up in Canada."

"Well, he must have had tryouts at his old school. I bet he had to go through the same kind of killer sessions," said Randy.

"That's true, Randy," Allison commented. It's funny that the two of them are such good friends. Randy is like fire, always getting worked up over things and saying exactly what she thinks about people. Allison is cool, like water. She always thinks carefully about every-thing before doing or saying anything. Randy says they're good for each other, and that Allison gives her another way of thinking about things.

Sometimes I think Sabs and I are like that, too. She's got so many friends and she's so popular. I have a lot of friends, but I'm not as open with people as she is, so we complement each other.

"So what are you guys doing here?" I asked again.

"Oh, we were just . . . uh . . . just . . .just." Randy began.

Mrs. Wells suddenly came into the kitchen, carrying a piece of paper. "Oh, girls, I found that menu. I knew I had it somewhere." She looked up and stopped short as soon as she saw me standing there. "Oh," she said, giving Sabs the same up-and-down-eyebrow look that Sabs had given Randy. "I didn't hear you girls come in." Crumpling the paper, Mrs. Wells. shoved it into her pocket and just stood there with her mouth open.

Sabs looked helplessly at Randy and Allison, who in turn stared at Mrs. Wells. What in the world was going on, I wondered.

"Do you want a cookie, Katie?" Mrs. Wells finally asked, pushing a tin full of homemade chocolate chunk cookies toward me.

"I shouldn't spoil my dinner," I said as I reached for a cookie anyway. I have a definite sweet tooth when it comes to cookies.

"Mom!" Sabs suddenly exclaimed. "There's a new boy in school. He's from Canada and speaks French. He's really cute and his name is Michel Beauvais."

"Really," Mrs. Wells said, sitting down at the kitchen table. "You know, I remember when I was in high school, this boy moved here from Canada. Pierre Montclair. Was he dreamy." Mrs. Wells got this faraway look on her face.

"Dreamy," Sabs mouthed at me, sitting down next to her mother. I fought the urge to giggle.

"Anyway, this was before I started going with your father, of course," her mother went on. "He had this incredible French accent — just the way he said my name used to make my knees weak."

"What happened?" Randy asked bluntly.

Mrs. Wells's eyes lost that glazed look, and she suddenly focused in on the four of us sitting around the table.

"Oh, well," Mrs. Wells said, standing up and straightening her shirt. "He moved back to Canada, I met your father, and the rest is history. Anyway, enough of that. Who's staying for dinner?"

My mom doesn't usually like me to have dinner out on a weeknight. But I really didn't feel like leaving Sabs's yet, especially since I still hadn't found out what was going on. So I called my mother. She wasn't home, so I left a message.

"That's really weird," I said to my friends after I hung up the phone.

"What is?" Sabs asked, pulling silverware out of the drawer next to the sink.

"No one's answering the phone at my house," I replied, sitting down. "That's the third time in two weeks my mom's been working late."

"Well, my mom's not home, either," Randy said, carrying five glasses into the dining room. "She's at some gallery in Minneapolis."

"I've got to get going," Allison said softly, putting on her coat. "Tonight's my father's birthday, and I've got to get home."

"Okay, Al," I said. "See you tomorrow."

"Bye, Allison," Sabs called.

Randy walked over and opened the door for Allison. She whispered something to Al, who looked right at me. Then Randy slipped her a piece of paper.

"*Ciao*, Allison," Randy said loudly. "See you *mañana*."

I opened my mouth again to ask what was going on, but Sabs cut me off. "So what's so weird about your mom not being home?" Maybe she had some shopping to do," she said, sitting down across from me.

Mrs. Wells came into the kitchen and put a big pot of water on the stove. "Spaghetti okay?" she asked us.

"Definitely!" Randy exclaimed. Randy loves home-cooked meals, since she and her mom end up eating a lot of takeout food.

"I can't believe my mom's not home again," I said.

"Well, there's no crime in working late," Randy retorted immediately. "Maybe it means

22

her job is going really well or something."

"I guess," I replied slowly. "I'm just not used to her working so much."

Suddenly Sam and his best friends, Jason and Nick, burst through the back door. "Spaghetti! Psych!" Sam exclaimed, after inhaling deeply.

"Great, I'm in for dinner!" Nick added, plopping down in the chair next to me. "So, Katie, are you guys ready for the Mongols?"

"Oh, yeah, the big game," Sam said, turning toward me. "Are you pumped?"

"We'll be ready," I answered confidently "And we got this new player today. He's Canadian."

"Canadian?" Jason asked, pushing Sabs over so he could share her chair. "He must be great!"

"He is," I replied. If nothing else, it was clear that Michel was a terrific hockey player. "And if Minneapolis doesn't know we have him, we'll have that much more of an advantage."

"Cool," Sam said, reaching for a cookie.

"Sam!" Sabs practically yelled, slapping his hand. "You have to have dinner first!"

"You're not my mother!" Sam shot back, snitching a cookie and shoving it in his mouth.

Sabs stuck her tongue out at her twin. I laughed. The two of them are so funny. Sam and Sabs may bicker a lot, but Sam is the first one to defend Sabs if someone picks on her. And sometimes, because they're twins, I really think they can read each other's minds.

"So, how old is this new guy on the hockey team?" Jason asked, brushing a lock of brown hair out of his eyes.

"He's in seventh grade like us," Sabs answered, before I could even get my mouth open. "And is he cute!"

"Who cares what he looks like?" Nick cut in with a frown. I think Nick has a crush on Sabs, even though he'll never come out and admit it. At the beginning of the year, he asked her to the Homecoming Dance, and now he really hates it when she talks about other guys. That's a definite giveaway, if you ask me.

We continued to talk about Bradley's chances of winning the hockey game until dinner was ready. Then Mr. Wells came home. Eating at the Wellses' is always an adventure. Since there are so many people, you really have to speak up or you won't even be heard. Dinner at my house is totally different. My mom always asks my sister and me about what's going on in school and stuff, but it's all much quieter than at the Wellses' house.

It wasn't until I was walking home after dinner that I started thinking about how much my mother had been working lately. It wasn't bad or anything — just different. I'm used to her always being home by the time I get in from practice, but lately she's not always there.

Then I remembered how strange everyone had acted when I walked into Sabs's kitchen. When the boys had burst in and everyone sat down to dinner, I'd never had a chance to find out what Sabs, Randy, and Allison were up to. I knew something was going on with them, and I intended to find out exactly what it was tomorrow.

Chapter Three

"So where is this French heart-throb?" Randy asked Sabs the next morning as the three of us stood by the locker Sabs and I share.

"I don't know," Sabs practically wailed. "I haven't seen him yet today, but I should have at least one class with him. Do you think he might have stayed home from school or something?"

I shook my head. "I doubt it," I replied, grabbing my books and shutting the locker. "We've got practice after school. He'd never miss that."

"Hey, Al," Randy called down the hall as Allison walked toward us. "Hurry up! We'll be late for class."

"Hi, guys," Allison replied, stopping in front of us. "Sorry, but I had to return a book to the library."

"Let's go, let's go," Sabs urged, starting off down the hall. "Maybe he's in our homeroom."

"Maybe he dropped out and moved back to Canada," Randy said, grinning.

"Oh, I hope not!" Sabs exclaimed, taking Randy's remark seriously. "I would just die."

"You would not," I reprimanded her. "He's just a boy." Sabs has a tendency to be dramatic. She says it's because she wants to be an actress. I am just the opposite. My father used to tell me that he knew he never had to worry about me because my feet are planted so firmly on the ground.

"His accent is to *die* for!" I heard Stacy Hansen exclaim, cutting into my thoughts.

Stacy is one of the most popular girls at school, and her father also happens to be the principal of our junior high school. Every time I see Stacy, who thinks she's just the cat's pajamas — to use my mother's words — I can't believe that I used to be part of her crowd. But that was last year, before my best friend, Erica, moved to California. And before I became friends with Sabs and met Randy and Allison. I really don't like Stacy at all, which is pretty serious for me, since I usually like most people.

"He *is* totally awesome!" Eva Malone agreed with her best friend. That was no surprise, since

Eva always agrees with Stacy no matter what.

"It doesn't look as if your French heartthrob stayed home, Sabs," Randy said, grinning at her. "It's not like Bradley gets a lot of awesome guys with *dreamy* accents every day. So who else could Stacy the Great be talking about?" Just then Randy flipped her black hair over her shoulder the way Stacy always flips her honey-blond hair, and gave a breathy giggle. We all laughed.

To say that Randy and Stacy don't get along is a major understatement. They fight all the time. Stacy acts as if she can get away with any-thing — and she usually does. Of course, Randy never gets away with anything.

"Oh, my gosh!" Sabs exclaimed, just as the warning bell sounded. "We'd better hurry!"

We slipped into the classroom before the final bell rang. Luckily, our English teacher, Ms. Staats, wasn't there yet.

I opened my notebook and uncapped a pen.

"Hi, guys!" Ms. Staats called as she breezed into the classroom. She isn't like a lot of the other teachers at Bradley. She wears cat's-eye glasses, for one thing, and as Randy always says, "She treats us like people."

Throwing her briefcase on the desk, Ms. Staats took attendance quickly. Then we listened to Mr. Hansen make the typical morning homeroom announcements. I have to admit I wasn't really paying attention until Mr. Hansen said something about our upcoming game. Then I couldn't stop thinking about the game. We just had to win. It was a major deal. Thinking about the hockey game made me start thinking about Michel. Shaking my head, I tried to put him out of my mind. So what if his accent was "dreamy," and he was kind of cute. I still wasn't sure how he felt about my being on the team.

"Okay, class," Ms. Staats said, opening and closing the book she had pulled out of her briefcase. "I hope you all finished reading *A Separate Peace.*"

The class groaned as everybody pulled out copies of the book. Luckily, I had finished it over the weekend. Looking over at Sabs, I saw her mouthing something to me. I wondered if she'd finished the assignment.

"Good!" Ms. Staats went on, ignoring the class's outburst. "So we can talk about it today. We'll be having an exam on the book next

Tuesday."

The class groaned again.

"What did you think of the ending, Sabrina?" Ms. Staats asked, smiling at Sabs.

I could see Sabs gulping from across the room. "Well . . . uh . . . I . . ." Sabs began, obviously struggling.

Suddenly someone knocked on the door. Sabs let out a huge breath of air. When Ms. Staats went to open the door, Sabs spun toward me.

"Katie!" she called whisper. "What do I think of the ending?"

I almost laughed. How was I supposed to know what she thought of the ending?

"He *is* cute!" Randy exclaimed in surprise from the back row.

I turned my attention toward the front of the room. Michel had just walked in the door and was talking to Ms. Staats.

"Class," Ms. Staats began, "this is Michel Beauvais. I hope you will all join me in welcoming him to Bradley Junior High. Why don't you have a seat, Michel?"

Of course, the only empty desk in the room happened to be right next to me.

"Bonjour, K. C.," Michel whispered as he slid into his chair. "I am glad that we are in a class together."

I just nodded. Fortunately for Sabs, Ms. Staats called on Jason instead to answer her question about the ending of *A Separate Peace.* But then she realized that Michel didn't have a copy of the book. And guess who he had to share with? Me.

"What do you have next hour?" Michel asked softly, after he moved his desk next to mine.

I have to admit it, his accent was really "dreamy."

"Lunch," I answered him in a whisper, trying to keep my mind on Ms. Staats's discussion of the assignment.

"Bon," he replied. "Good. So do I. May I eat with you?"

I looked up and saw Sabs making those funny motions with her eyebrows again. It was obvious that she had overheard Michel, and she wanted to make sure that I told him it was okay. What was I supposed to say, no? I swear Sabs has radar sometimes. She manages to pick up on news and gossip even if it's happening all the way on the other side of the room.

"Sure," I managed to get out. Maybe it wouldn't be so bad. Maybe he had just been surprised to find a girl on the team and didn't really have a problem with it.

After class, Michel and I waited for Randy, Sabs and Allison. I introduced Randy and Allison.

"K. C., I have to go to my locker first," Michel said as we started down the hall toward the cafeteria. "I will meet you there." He pointed in the totally opposite direction from the one we were walking in.

Sabs giggled. "Actually, the cafeteria is that way," she said, pointing the way we were going.

"Aayyy!" Michel exclaimed. "I am never going to figure this place out! Don't worry, I'll meet you there." With that, he turned and ran down the hall.

As usual, the cafeteria was packed when we got there.

"There's a table!" Randy called out over her shoulder. And she started walking toward the table.

"K.C.!" someone yelled as we passed the

hockey table. As usual, most of the guys were wearing their black-and-orange hockey jackets. They never take them off — even inside. I don't have one yet, since the captain usually gives them out at the end of the season.

"How's it going, guys?" I asked the table in general.

"Don't forget to load up on carbs this week," Scottie said, eyeing the yogurt, apple, and milk on my tray. I don't really like eating a big lunch. It always makes me feel too full for the rest of the day.

"Don't worry about it," I said. "I had pasta last night."

"Cool," Flip replied. "We've got to be totally ready for the Mongols!"

"Why don't you sit down?" Scottie asked me with a smile. A lock of blond hair fell over his eyes, and he brushed it back absently. I must say that Scottie Silver is really cute. I blushed, remembering how he had once kissed me on the cheek when I had tried out for the team. We've gone to the movies a few times since then, but he's never kissed me again.

I shook my head and told them I'd see them at practice. Then I headed toward the table where my friends were already sitting. I guess they were so busy talking that they didn't hear me come up, because Allison dropped her sandwich in surprise when I sat down. They all stopped talking at once and suddenly seemed to get really interested in their lunches. Weird. Something was definitely up.

"What is going on?" I asked, remembering that none of them had answered my questions from the night before when they were acting so strangely.

"What are you talking about?" Randy countered, not meeting my eyes.

"I'm talking about —" I started to say.

"Michel!" Sabs shouted, jumping up and cutting me off. "We're over here!"

I saw Michel smile in our direction from the other side of the cafeteria. Then he started walking toward us.

"Hey, dude," Scottie called from the hockey table. "Sit with us!" He waved at Michel.

"*Je suis dèsolè*," Michel answered. "I'm sorry, but I promised K.C. I would eat with her." He motioned to where we were sitting.

I noticed Scottie glare at Michel and then at me. What was his problem? It was only lunch.

"Allo," Michel said, sitting down across from me. Then he looked at my lunch. "K. C., you should be eating more than that. We have a big game coming up."

"I know," I replied a little shortly. I always eat the same things for lunch — either a peanut butter and jelly sandwich or a yogurt. "Don't worry, I'll be fine."

Michel shook his head, not looking at all convinced. "Okay, K. C.."

"So, how do you like Acorn Falls so far?" Sabs asked, taking a sip of her lemon-lime seltzer. Sabs says that sparkling water is the thing to drink now. She claims that soda and stuff like that are out.

It was obvious to me that Michel had definitely becomes Sabs's next crush. But he seemed to like her, too, so I figured that was okay.

As the five of us talked and joked around, I decided that Michel was actually an okay kind of guy. He even admitted that when he found out I was a girl, he hadn't meant to be rude, but he had been completely surprised that a girl was on the hockey team. He explained that he had no problem with it, but that girls in Canada have their own hockey teams. So it was just very different.

Anyway, lunch practically flew by. And I have to admit we all had a good time hanging out with Michel — including me.

Chapter Four

Coach Budd worked us really hard at practice that afternoon. I guess he wanted to make sure we were totally ready for the big game — even if it killed us!

We started with a half hour of wind sprints. Wind sprints are where we skate as fast as we can in one direction, and then the coach blows his whistle, and we change direction and skate as fast as we can the other way. Then we scrimmaged for an hour and a half straight. It was total torture.

After practice, I walked home very slowly. I was exhausted. My equipment bag felt as if it were filled with rocks. Even though my arms were ready to fall off, I was starting to get psyched about the game. But then, strangely, I began to miss my dad. I really wished he were alive, so he could come to my game. I knew that he would be as excited about it as I was. And I knew that he would be really proud of me. It's strange. My dad's been dead for three years, and I don't think about him nearly as much as I used to, but then all of a sudden I just start missing him.

My eyes started to tear as I turned up my driveway. I paused outside my house, blinking furiously. My mom's car was in the driveway, and I saw a light in the kitchen. I didn't want to walk in bawling. I took a deep, shaky breath to calm myself. I hate for anyone to see me cry — especially my mom or my sister. I know they miss Dad, too, and I don't think it's good for them to see me upset.

A few minutes later, I opened the front door. I could smell lasagna cooking. I love lasagna, but my mom doesn't make it all that often anymore because it takes so long to prepare. I wondered what the occasion was.

"Mom?" I called as I walked into the living room. I dropped my equipment bag on the rose-colored carpet. I knew that my mom would yell at me to put it in the back closet, as she always does, but I was just too tired to carry it any farther.

There were fresh flowers on top of the piano,

the coffee table, and the end tables on both sides of the couch. When my father was alive, my mother always kept a ton of vases full of flowers around the house. My father often said that flowers cheered everything up. But I hadn't seen this many flowers in the house for years. I wondered what was going on.

"Mom?" I called again, still not getting any reply. I headed back to the kitchen, but then I stopped short right outside. Unbelievable. The radio was on. Since Dad died, Mom had pretty much only listened to the news station. But I definitely heard music coming from the kitchen. Mozart, I thought.

"Are you in here?" I asked, pushing the kitchen door open. As I peeked around the corner, my mouth dropped open in shock. My mother was waltzing around the kitchen with a wooden spoon in her hand. But that wasn't the end of it. She looked absolutely gorgeous!

She had on a new red dress with matching pumps, and her nails were polished the same shade of red! Her hair had been cut, permed, and highlighted a brighter shade of blond. And she was even wearing red lipstick that matched her dress.

"What did you do to yourself?" I asked in shock.

"Do you like it, honey?" she said, patting her hair. "I felt it was time for a change. I took a half day from work to get my hair done and do some shopping."

My mouth dropped open again. I stared at this younger-looking, more fashionable woman who was pretending to be my mother. "Uh ... yes ... Mom," I answered. "You look great!" And she did. She just didn't look like my mom. Usually my mother wears navy blue or gray suits to work, and her hair is always pulled tightly off her face in a bun. And she never wears pumps, or takes off from work early to go shopping!

Smiling again, my mother opened the oven to check the lasagna. "Well, I'm glad you like it, Katie. We've got another twenty minutes until dinner, so why don't you go ahead and start your homework. By the way, did you put your hockey bag in the hall closet?"

At least this fashion plate still *sounded* like my mother, I though with some relief. Shaking my head, I put it in the closet and headed upstairs. I felt kind of dazed.

"Katie," Emily whispered from the doorway of her bedroom, which is across the hall from my room. "Come here."

I could tell from her panicked tone of voice that she must have seen Mom, too. I threw my books in my room and went over to her. Quickly, Emily pulled me inside and shut the door.

"Did you see Mom?" Emily asked in a hushed tone.

I flopped down on her white lace comforter and nodded silently. Emily paced back and forth across the room. I was surprised. My sister is definitely not the type to pace — ever. Emily is sixteen and the captain of the high school varsity pompom squad. She has long blond hair and gorgeous bone structure, and everything about her is always perfect. We're very different, but we're learning how to get along with each other better. I mean, when I quit the flag squad to join the hockey team, I thought she'd never get over it. She couldn't understand how I could possibly want to play hockey instead of being a flag girl as she'd been when she was my age. But now she's okay about it.

"Yeah, I saw her," I said finally. I don't know

why, but I felt that if we just didn't *talk* about the way Mom looked, she would transform back into her old self by the time we went down to dinner.

"Well?" Emily asked impatiently, her voice rising a little. She turned to face me and put her hands on her hips. "What do you think?"

"I don't know if red is her color," I began, and then stopped. I didn't know what else to say. I didn't really like my mother looking so ... so ... young and fashionable. But I couldn't tell Emily that. It was too stupid and selfish to say aloud.

"Is that all you have to say?" Emily demanded, absently twisting the gold bracelet that her boyfriend, Reed, had given her last year for Christmas. The two of them are the perfect All-American couple — the captain of the football team and the head of the pompom squad.

"Well, what do you want me to say?" I asked, a little shortly.

"Something must be up," Emily continued, ignoring me. "Mom wouldn't take off from work to get her hair and nails done just for the heck of it. And did you see all of those flowers all over the living room?

"Well?" Emily asked. "Don't you think something's up?

I nodded unhappily. If something was up, I'd really rather not know about it. But Mom was dancing around the kitchen in a brand-new dress and heels. There was definitely something up.

"We've got to find out what, or who, made her change her hair and buy new clothes and miss work," Emily said, sitting down next to me. "Right?"

I looked down at my hands without answering her. I couldn't help feeling that maybe it was none of our business. But of course I couldn't say that to Emily, either.

"Girls!" my mother called up the stairs. "Dinner!"

"Right?" Emily repeated, a bit more firmly.

I nodded glumly as I kicked my sneaker into Emily's pale blue carpeting.

"Let's go!" Mom called again.

I went to wash up for dinner. When I got downstairs, I saw the Mom had decided we would eat in the dining room for a change. Now I was definitely starting to get worried.

As soon as Emily saw me, she opened her

eyes really wide and raised her eyebrows at the bowl of fresh flowers in the middle of the table.

"Would you get the salad, Katie?" Mom asked, coming through the dining room door with a steaming pan of lasagna. I jumped up, startled, and quickly headed back into the kitchen. I hoped that Mom hadn't seen Emily making those faces at me.

Finally, we all sat down to eat.

"So, Mom," Emily began, staring intently into her salad. "How was your day?" She speared a piece of lettuce and shoved the whole thing into her mouth. Emily was obviously upset. She never eats like that.

Mom smiled. "I've already told you that I've had a great day, Emily," she said in this bubble voice I hadn't heard in ages. "How'd your day go, honey?"

"It was fine," Emily replied, frowning into her plate. I could tell she was getting frustrated. I was, too. Why had Mom given herself such a major make-over? What was the big secret? She was being almost as mysterious as Sabs, Al, and Randy. Which reminded me, I'd have to bug them tomorrow and make them explain all the whispering and secret looks they kept giving one another.

"Did you have a good day, Katie?" Mom asked, flashing a big smile in my direction.

"Mom," I began, ignoring her question, "why'd you change your hair?"

"I thought you said you liked it," my mother replied, her smile fading a little. "You do like it, don't you?"

"Oh, yeah, I like it," I reassured her. I kicked Emily under the table. She should support Mom, too.

"You look great, Mom," Emily added, still not looking up from her dinner.

"Good," Mom said, smiling widely again. "I really don't know. I just thought it was time for something new. I can't even remember the last time I changed my hair."

"It was the year before Dad died," Emily said quickly. "You got it cut really short right before you both went to Jamaica. Remember? You hated it and swore you'd never cut it again."

I winced and shot a glance at my mother, but she was calmly eating her lasagna. She didn't seem to have noticed Emily's obnoxious tone of voice at all.

"So, Katie, are you ready for your big game this weekend?" Mom asked, changing the subject.

It's really weird. At first, Mom didn't want me to try out for the hockey team. But now that I'm on the team, she's one of our biggest fans. She has come to practically every game, even the out-of-town games. I think the idea of ice hockey reminded her too much of my dad. He played semi pro, and he lived and breathed the sport. It's no wonder I feel as if it's in my blood.

"How's work going?" Emily asked, switching tactics. She was obviously going to keep asking Mom questions until she told us why she had gotten this make-over — no matter how long it took.

"Good," my mother said, taking a sip of water. "In fact, it's really good. It must be the time of year to buy a house, because I'm doing more mortgages than ever. And so many new customers. I approved a mortgage last week for a very nice man who just moved to town. He closed on his house yesterday."

Emily shot me a glance and raised her eyebrows again.

"Anyone want more water?" Mom asked,

standing up and holding her empty glass.

Emily and I shook our heads and watched silently as she walked out of the dining room.

"See!" Emily hissed as soon as the kitchen door swung shut.

"See what?" I asked, a little confused. So business was good, what did that mean?

"Katie, don't be so thick," Emily retorted. "Mom met a man!"

"Right, she approved some guy's mortgage," I said, still confused.

"Katie!" Emily exclaimed impatiently. "Mom never talks about the people she gives mortgages to, just the number of mortgages and loans."

Just then the kitchen door swung open, and Mom walked back into the dining room. I wondered, as I watched her sit down, if she could tell we had been talking about her.

Thinking about what Emily had said, I tried to keep talking to Mom normally. Emily was right. Mom must have met a man. Could he be the reason she'd given herself this make-over, filled the house with flowers, and been dancing around the kitchen?

"Oh, by the way," my mother began, as we

cleared the table after dinner, "I'd like both of you to be home early for dinner on Sunday. I invited that nice man I met at the bank over for dinner."

She said it all casually, but I felt as if I couldn't breathe. My mom was looking at me expectantly. All I could do was nod. What I really wanted to do was scream, but I didn't, of course. Mom, Emily, and I are all really good at not showing how upset we are about stuff, but this was truly terrible. Mom couldn't have a boyfriend! I felt as if my world was coming apart.

Chapter Five

My room was still dark when I woke up on Saturday morning. I squinted at the clock — only six-thirty. I didn't have to be at the rink until one, but I knew I couldn't stay in bed any longer. This was too big a game. It was the biggest game of the year. If we beat the Minneapolis Mongols this afternoon, we'd make the state playoffs for the first time ever.

Not able to sit still another second, I practically jumped out of bed. My cat, Pepper, meowed her protest at the movement. Pepper sleeps with me every night.

Digging my toes into my fluffy powder-blue carpet, I paused for a moment to stretch. What was I going to do for five and a half hours, I wondered. I grabbed my robe and walked downstairs.

I pushed open the kitchen door and stopped short in the doorway. There was a big package sitting in the middle of the kitchen table. I walked closer and saw a card with my name written on it. I opened the card.

Dear Katie,
Happy Early Birthday!
Good luck today. I am very proud of you
and I know your father would be, too.
Love, Mom

My fingers were shaking as I opened the box. It was definitely the right size for what I wanted, but still, you never know. I never jump to conclusions. That way, I never get disappointed.

Flipping the lid off, I sat down with my mouth open. Inside the box was a pair of brand-new hockey skates! They were gorgeous! Mom had even put in orange laces to match our orange-and-black uniforms. I picked one up and hugged it. I wanted to call Sabs to tell her about them, but I knew she wouldn't be up for hours yet.

Still holding the skate, I ran upstairs to take a shower and get dressed. In no time flat, I was all set to go.

I stopped in the kitchen to pick up the other skate and write my mom a note to say thank you and tell her where I was going. I glanced at the clock, and it read seven-fifteen. Emily and Mom were still sleeping, so I didn't want to bother them. Grabbing my hockey stick out of the closet, I shoved a puck in my pocket. I almost forgot my gloves and hat and had to go back for them. But finally I was on my way to Elm Park.

Before Dad died, he and I would get up early on Saturday mornings and go skating at Elm Park pond. It was a ritual for us. I still go skating there sometimes, even though it makes me miss him. I always get the feeling that he would be glad to know that I'm still skating there. So that makes me happy.

The cold air felt good against my face, and I started to get excited about the game. As I got closer to the pond, I realized that someone else was already skating there. Who in the world would be up this early, I wondered. My heart sank a little. I really wanted to be alone this particular morning.

Heading for the bench at the side of the pond, I noticed a red scarf with white Canadian maple leaves on it. I recognized that scarf. Sitting down and pulling off my boots, I stared at the skater on the ice. No wonder I thought I knew that scarf — it was Michel's.

"Bon matin, K. C.," Michel said, coming to a stop in front of the bench. "Good morning. Ah, *bien*. Good. You have new skates."

"Aren't they nice?" I asked as I finished lacing them. "My mom gave them to me for my birthday." I stood up.

"I though your birthday wasn't for another week," Michel said, skating backwards slowly.

My eyes narrowed. "How do you know when my birthday is?" I asked him suspiciously. I knew that I hadn't said anything about it to anyone.

"Ah . . . uh . . ." Michel began, stopping suddenly. ". . . I . . . Sabs must have told me."

"Oh," I replied. I guess that made sense. If Sabs told the whole school when her birthday was, why wouldn't she tell everyone about mine? I did a short cross over turn. The skates felt great. No one was going to catch me today.

"What are you doing out here so early?" Michel asked, changing the subject. He began doing figure eights on one foot and then the other.

"I was . . . uh . . . kind of nervous," I said,

stuttering a little. I hadn't meant to admit that to him, since he didn't seem like the type who got flustered like that before a game. But it just sort of slipped out.

"Me too," Michel replied, grinning at me. "I miss skating outside also. We used to have a pond in front of our house. I skated on it all the time."

"Wow!" I said, impressed. That would be awesome. Imagine being able to skate any time of the day on your own private pond. "It must have been really hard for you to move here," I finished.

Michel nodded. "It was. I had a lot of friends at home. And my hockey team was *incroyable*, I mean incredible! We have been regional champions for the last eight years."

"We're not bad, you know!" I replied a little defensively. We weren't either. Just because we weren't champs or anything for the last how ever many years didn't mean we weren't going to be.

Michel laughed. "Oh, this team is not bad at all, K. C.," he replied. "In fact, this team is pretty good. Of course, they couldn't beat my team."

"What?!" I exclaimed angrily before I realized that he was just joking. I giggled. "Besides, we are your team now."

Looking thoughtful, Michel nodded. "I guess that's true," he said slowly. Then he laughed. "And we are going to make the play-offs today, right?"

"Right," I agreed emphatically. As I pushed the puck around on the ice, I started getting very psyched. I thought we had a good chance before, but now that we had Michel on our team, we were going to whip the Mongols!

Michel and I skated around for about half an hour, before I flopped back down on the bench. "I guess I should get going," I said, reluctantly. "I don't want to get tired before the game."

"Good idea," Michel agreed. "Besides, I am hungry!"

"What time is it?" I asked suddenly.

"Eight-thirty," Michel replied, sitting down next to me to take off his skates. "Why?"

"Sabrina, Allison, and Randy are coming over for brunch at nine-thirty," I said. "I'd better get moving."

"Your friends are very nice, K. C.," Michel said, pulling on his boots. "And so are you. I am glad to have met such nice people so soon."

I blushed a little at his compliment, remembering what I had thought of Michel when I had first met him. It's so true what they say about first impressions. It really isn't fair to judge people like that.

"You are a very good skater," Michel went on.

"Thanks," I replied, tying my skates together and standing up. Michel finished tying his boots and got up, too. We started walking out of the park, "My dad taught me to skate."

"He must be very good. Does he play hockey, too?" Michel asked, hanging his skates over the end of his stick and balancing the stick on his shoulder.

Even after all this time, I'm still not used to it. Sometimes, when people mention my father, it just makes me want to cry. "My dad died three years ago," I said quietly.

"I am so sorry," Michel apologized. "I didn't know."

"How could you?" I asked reasonably. "Don't worry about it."

We walked out of the park in silence. Michel turned to go toward Maple Street, and I turned toward my house.

"I'll see you at the rink at twelve!" I called out over my shoulder.

"Okay," he called back. "And make sure you eat enough!"

Laughing, I trudged home. The guys on the team are always trying to tell me what to do. And now Michel, too. He fitted right in without even trying.

I opened the back door as quietly as I could and dropped my skates and stuff by the door. I hoped my mother and my sister were up already.

Stepping into the house, I smelled bacon cooking. Pausing, I took a deep breath. This had always been my favorite part of skating with my father — coming home to breakfast with my family. It was great to come in from the cold to a warm kitchen and the smell of bacon and coffee, and to sit down with my folks for the morning.

I practically ran into the kitchen. My mom was standing in front of the stove, spatula in her hand. She was wearing a new pale blue sweater that matched her blue eyes perfectly.

Going over and giving her a big hug, I cried,

"Thanks, Mom! I love them!"

Mom hugged me. Then she stepped away and brushed the hair out of my eyes. "I'm glad you like the skates, honey," she said softly. "So, what time are the girls going to be here?"

"Oh, my gosh, they'll be here any minute! I'd better go get cleaned up!"

"Okay, Katie," said Mom, turning back to the stove. "And please wake up your sister. We don't want to be late for your game."

I paused at the door. I couldn't believe how great that made me feel. I had no idea my mother and sister would turn out to be such great hockey fans. I ran up to my room and quickly changed out of my skating clothes. I hopped into the shower again and was getting into my powder-blue sweats when the doorbell rang.

"I'll get it, Mom!" I called, running downstairs to answer the front door.

"Hey," said Randy, stepping inside. "How's it going?"

I took her black leather bomber jacket and hung it in the front closet. Randy was wearing leopard-print cotton leggings, an oversized black sweater, and her ever-present black granny boots. As I said, she dresses really cool because she's from New York. I love her clothes, but they are definitely not my style.

"So, are you nervous about the game?" Randy asked, following me into the kitchen.

"A little," I admitted. "But I'm sure I'll be fine as soon as we start playing."

"I know you guys are definitely going to rock today," Randy stated confidently. "Don't worry about it. Hey, Mrs. C!"

"Hi, Randy," my mom replied with a smile. "How are you this morning?"

"Cool," Randy said, plopping down in one of the kitchen chairs.

It took my mom a while to get used to Randy, but no Mom practically loves her.

"What kind of pancakes do you want, Randy?" Mom asked, waving her spatula around.

"What do you have?" Randy wanted to know.

"Apple, cinnamon, blueberry, strawberry, or chocolate chip," my mom replied, gesturing to all the bowls of ingredients on the counter next to the stove.

"Definitely chocolate chip," Randy replied, leaning back in her chair. "Breakfast is definitely one of my favorite meals — especially when someone makes it!"

My mom shot me an "I told you so" glance. She's always saying that Randy would be better off if Mrs. Zak cooked more instead of always having takeout food.

The doorbell rang again, and I went to let Allison in. Sabs showed up a few minutes later.

After we gorged ourselves on Mom's pancakes, we collapsed in the den for an hour, watching cartoons and talking. Before I knew it, it was time to get ready for the big game. I was definitely starting to get nervous. I just hoped the butterflies in my stomach would go away once we started playing, as I had told Randy. But right then I felt too nervous even to tie my skate laces.

Chapter Six

"Nice skates, K.C.," Flip said as he passed the puck to me an hour later. The whole team was on the ice warming up. Everyone was more than a little hyper about this game. I, for one, couldn't wait to get started.

"Thanks," I called back, doing a few crossover turns.

"Did your new frog friend give them to you?" Scottie asked snidely, spraying ice on my legs as he skated to a stop in front of me.

"Scottie," Flip said, as if he was warning him.

"I want to know," Scottie replied, his eyes practically boring holes into mine.

Scottie can be pretty obnoxious sometimes. In fact, he's been very obnoxious to me in the past. But I had never seen him like this.

"What are you talking about?" I demanded. Why was he acting like such a jerk? Maybe he was just nervous or something. But I didn't really think so. Games didn't usually make him so crazy. I thought it had to be something else.

"I knew it," Scottie declared, skating away. What was going on? How was I supposed to concentrate on the game when Scottie was acting like this?

I shot a glance at Flip, but he just shrugged. I didn't have time to say anything else because at that moment the coach blew his whistle to call us all over to the bench. That meant we were going to start in only a few minutes.

I could feel the team's excitement as we squeezed onto the bench. I sat between Flip and Michel. Everyone was ready to go out there onto the ice and start playing. I was trying to get my mind back on the game and off Scottie when Coach Budd started his pregame pep talk.

"Team," he began, "this is a big game today. But you're up for it. You've worked hard and you're ready."

The team cheered. We all knew that we had definitely worked hard. I looked over at Scottie at the other end of the bench to find him glaring at me. I shook my head and stared out at the ice,trying to focus. I closed my eyes for a second and thought of my dad and how he had always said that if I tried I would succeed. He said that the most important thing was to have will. I supposed that I had will. He had always said I did.

The referee's whistle brought me back to the present. It was time to start the game. And I was ready.

"Those guys look huge!" Flip exclaimed as the Mongols hit the ice. "They can't be junior high kids!"

"*Flip!*" the coach screamed. "None of that kind of talk! They're just kids like you guys, and there's nothing special about them."

"Except that they've been state champs for practically forever," Flip muttered, pulling on his helmet.

"Yeah, and check out their goalie's mask," Brian added under his breath. The goalie had a monster face painted on his mask. It definitely looked intimidating.

"Now let's get out there and win!" Coach Budd yelled.

Tightening my helmet strap, I skated slowly out to my position at left wing.

"*Bonne chance*, K. C.!" Michel called from

right behind me. "Good luck!"

"*Merci*," I replied, turning around and grinning. Michel smiled and winked at me.

Pivoting, I faced Scottie. He wasn't even looking at the Mongols as they took the ice. Scottie was staring at me and Michel with this big sneer on his face instead!

The Mongols gave off a very professional image with their red, white, and blue uniforms. They looked like a national team or something.

Practically growling, the Mongols' right wing suddenly stopped about three feet in front of me. Curling his lip, he glared at me as if he was trying to stare me down. Not even blinking, I glared back. My dad never let anyone intimidate him on the ice, and I wasn't about to either.

Suddenly I became aware of the crowd as everyone started roaring. The referee was about to drop the puck to start the game. I looked around the stand, trying to spot my mom and my friends. But there were just too many people.

Then the game started. Scottie shot a pass to Flip, and we were over the center line, heading toward the net. I remember thinking in one second that the Mongols were not as great as we thought they were going to be, then in the next I was flat on my back on the ice. Flip had passed to me, and I didn't even get to see the puck flying in my direction. I was checked by someone on the Mongol defense — or the Wall, as the defense is known. Then I hit the ice, hard.

The first period was pretty rough. The Mongols were definitely a physical team. We were getting checked all over the place. Which is not to say we weren't dishing anything out. They were hitting the boards, too. But we were definitely hitting the ice more than they were.

The Mongols' Wall was impenetrable. Nothing was getting through them. Forget about any player — not even the puck was getting by those guys.

But so far they hadn't managed to score, either. Michel was awesome! He was literally all over the place. He was really fast, and the Mongols never saw him coming. I remembered he had told me that they play a much more physical game in Canada than they do in Minnesota. I guess he was used to the way the Mongols were playing. I certainly wasn't. I felt as if I was getting beat up.

Our bench was pretty quiet when we sat down at the end of the first period. We were all gulping Gatorade and trying to catch our breath.

"Those guys are awesome!" Scottie said, shaking his head.

"You can't get through them," Flip added, wiping the sweat dripping off his forehead.

"You can't give up like that!" Coach Budd yelled.

"But you saw us out there," Brian said. "They're killing us!"

"Stop panicking!" Coach Budd instructed. "Otherwise, they will kill you."

"But ..." Flip began.

"Aayyy!" Michel suddenly exclaimed loudly. "Have some faith in yourselves! They haven't scored on us either!"

That shut us all up because we knew it was true.

The ref blew his whistle, signaling the beginning of the second period. We stood up.

"Now let's get out there and show 'em what got us here!" the coach yelled, slapping us all on the back as we filed past him onto the ice.

The Mongols got control of the puck and

began moving down the ice. Two of them sur-
rounded Michel and practically sandwiched
him into the boards. While he was out of com-
mission, the Mongols' center took a shot on goal
from fifteen feet out. It flew into the upper left-
hand corner of the net before anyone could
react, least of all Peter Mullins, our goalie.

The Mongols' fans went wild. The players
were slapping hands and whooping. Michel
was dragging himself up from the ice where he
had been pushed. I started to skate toward him
to help him up, when I felt someone tug on my
jersey. I spun around.

"What?" Scottie asked snidely. "Your
boyfriend need some help standing up?"

Pushing his hand away angrily, I skated
back to my position. Michel was not my
boyfriend! I had no idea why Scottie thought he
was. As we got set to face off again, I glared at
everyone. The Mongols' right wing stared at me
with a major grin on his face, but I must have
looked thunderous, because his smile faded.
Scottie was not going to get away with his
obnoxious behavior. And the Mongols were not
going to get away with their goal — not if I
could help it.

The Mongols got control of the puck again. The center set a hard pass to the right wing. He tried to move around me, but I was having none of that. I poked the puck away from him and shot it at a surprised Scottie about fifteen feet in front of their goalie.

Luckily, Scottie had quick reflexes. He grabbed the puck, pivoted, and faked a shot on goal. Pushing it around one of the members of the Wall, he took a clear, diagonal shot toward the goal. The goalie got a piece of it, and I thought it was going to end up in his glove. But he dropped it — right into the net!

"All right!" Flip shouted. "Way to go, K.C.! What a steal!"

"Nice shot, Silver!" Peter screamed from our goal.

Scottie started skating toward me, a triumphant grin on his face. Stopping short, he frowned at someone behind me.

"Aayyy!" Michel exclaimed, patting me on the back. "Nice move, K. C.. Very slick."

I smiled at him and looked back toward Scottie. But he had already turned away and was slapping hands with Flip. Before I had a chance to think about it further, we were lining up once more. The remaining minutes of the second period were fast and furious, but no one scored again. The Mongols were still playing with major physical intensity, but we must have been getting used to it. We didn't end up on the ice nearly as much as we had in the first period. I know I was bracing myself better when I saw one of the Mongols approaching.

Feeling battered and exhausted, I plopped on the bench between periods. Guzzling Gatorade, I ignored Scottie, who was sitting next to me. Actually, he was ignoring me anyway. I was just trying to catch my breath, so I hardly even notice.

Too soon, way too soon, the ref blew his whistle for the start of the third and final period. I dragged myself off the bench and practically hobbled out onto the ice. I had played most of the first two periods and expected more of a rest right then. I guess the coach wanted to stick with his starters, though. I was just so tired. I definitely did not feel nearly as up as I had at the beginning of the game.

The Mongols came back with a vengeance. I guess they weren't too happy about our goal. Actually, I think it was the steal that made them the maddest. They were all over me. Every time I stood up, I kept getting thrown into the boards by another red, white, and blue jersey.

I could tell that Michel was trying to help me out. But he couldn't really leave his zone, or they would score more goals. He frowned at me whenever I glanced his way, though.

The Mongols' right wing got the puck again. I moved in to try for another steal. We couldn't get anything going — but neither could they. The right wing was a little loose in his puck control, and I thought I had a good chance to get a piece of it. My stick finally hit the puck, and I fought for control of it. I was so busy concentrating on the right wing and the puck that I didn't even notice the center barreling toward me until it was too late.

He slammed me right into the boards. I hit the plastic guard — hard — and bounced off. The center had backed off, and I had nowhere else to fall but the ice. It all happened so fast, I didn't even have time to throw my arms up to break my fall. My face hit the ice first.

I must have blacked out for a moment. My first conscious thought was that my face felt sticky. I tried to sit up, but couldn't

"Katie?" someone said from close by. I turned my head a little and saw Scottie looking down at me, his green eyes dark with concern. "Katie, are you okay?"

I tried to nod, but I couldn't really move my head.

"Campbell?" Coach Budd asked brusquely.

Taking a deep breath, I pulled myself into a sitting position. The coach reached through the crowd and gently pushed me back down.

"Just lie still, Campbell," the coach ordered. He called to someone on the bench. "Kurt, go get the doc."

I must have looked really concerned after he said that. "Don't worry, Campbell. It's just a precaution," he hurried to reassure me.

"Wow!" Flip exclaimed at the same time that Michel said, *"Mon Dieu!"*

Shaking my hand, I tried to get my glove off. Scottie saw my problem and pulled it off for me. I touched my face. It was definitely sticky.

"What happened?" I asked, dazed. "I feel like I got run over by a truck."

Flip laughed. "You kind of look like it, too."

As soon as the team doctor saw me, he insisted I come down to the locker room so he could get a better look at me. I really wanted to watch the rest of the game, but after one glance at the doctor's face, I knew it was useless to argue.

"Are you okay?" the coach asked again, helping me to my feet.

I nodded, barely noticing the cheering of the crowd as I stood up. The coach pressed a towel to my lip.

"Looks like a split lip," the doctor said, looking at me more closely. "And your cheekbone is probably going to have a major bruise on it. To say nothing of your chin — that's really bleeding."

I put my hand to my face. The numbness was starting to wear off, and everything was beginning to hurt. As I walked off the ice, the game started again, with Brian playing left wing in my place. I could see Scottie. He was playing ferociously, checking anyone and everyone.

I was surprised to see my mom and Emily in the locker room. They both looked really worried.

"Mom, I'm okay," I managed to say, although my lip was already swelling up.

"Don't worry."

Mom looked a little relieved, until the doctor explained that I needed stitches in my chin. I guess she thought she was finished with stitches and stuff after I got older.

I was feeling kind of dopey by the time the doctor finished with me — he had given me a pain-killer before sewing the cut on my chin.

I don't remember much after that until I woke up later that night in my bed, wearing my pajamas. Moving, I groaned. I definitely felt as if a truck had run over me — and then backed up. And I knew it was only going to be worse in the morning.

Feeling a little groggy, I looked at the clock. It was ten o'clock. Then it hit me. I didn't even know who had won the game. How could I have slept all this time? How could I not have seen the end of the game?

I had to get up and find out. I tried to move my legs, but I was too sore. Then I tried to open my mouth to call Mom, but my lips were too swollen and my chin felt really stiff. I was exhausted from trying to move, so I gave up and fell back to sleep.

Chapter Seven

The sun woke me up on Sunday morning. Experimentally, I stretched. I groaned loudly. Every part of my body hurt. Then everything that had happened the day before came rushing back to me. The game, Scottie, that Mongol who had knocked me over, my stitches ... I touched the bandage on my chin.

But who won? I didn't even know who had won the game! I was going to have to get out of bed to find that out, at least. Moaning all the while, I dragged my legs to the side of the bed and sat up. I saw spots before my eyes. I sat on the side of the bed and tried to get my bearings. Once I could see clearly, I stood up. Big mistake. My muscles screamed for me to sit down again. But I was determined. Grabbing my robe, I headed downstairs.

No one was up yet. Glancing at the clock, I saw that it was only seven-thirty. Who could I call to ask about the game? Then it hit me that I might not even be able to talk because of the stitches in my chin. I walked over to the mirror in the front hall. When I saw my face, I was shocked. My left cheekbone was black and blue and puffy, my lips were totally swollen, and there was a huge white bandage on my chin. I looked as if I had been in a terrible car accident.

Just then something hit the front door, and I jumped. The Sunday paper, I thought happily. That was what just hit the front door. The paper would have the score from yesterday's game in the sports section. Then I grinned. Well, at least I could grin, but when I glanced back at the mirror, I have to admit that my expression resembled something much more like a horror-movie grimace than a human smile. Oh, well. I guessed it was just the price one had to pay for a good hockey game.

I opened the door and grabbed the heavy paper off the front mat. Walking back toward the kitchen, I fumbled with the rubber band. I felt as if I couldn't wait another second to find out if we were going to the playoffs.

Sitting down at the table, I opened the paper and searched frantically for the sports section.

There it was on the front page. We had won, 2–1! I couldn't believe it. I was just sitting there with this dumb smile on my face when my mother walked into the kitchen.

"Katie!" my mom exclaimed. "What are you doing out of bed?"

"Hi, Mom," I said, turning back to the paper. "I had to find out who won the game."

"Katie, you should get back into bed," Mom said, walking toward the refrigerator. "I'll bring you the newspaper and your breakfast up there. What do you want?"

"We won, Mom!" I said excitedly, not moving from my chair. Just knowing that we had won had made me forget all my aches and pains for the moment. We were going to the playoffs! I couldn't believe it. My dad would have been so proud!

"I know, honey," Mom replied. "All your friends called last night. They were happy we won, but everyone is worried sick about you."

"Everybody called last night?" I asked, confused. "I didn't hear the phone ring once."

My mom laughed gently. "You were kind of out of it, Katie," she said. "But, after Sabrina, Randy, and Allison called, I think the entire team called — even Coach Budd!"

"It's a great team, Mom," I said, with the biggest smile I could manage. "And best of all, we won!" I slowly turned back around in my chair to read the rest of the article.

"Katie, the doctor said that you should rest all day today," my mom said, walking toward me. "If you don't feel like being in your room, at least go lie down in the living room. You can eat breakfast in there. Okay?"

Mom was obviously not going to let up until I was lying down and resting. I nodded slowly, picked up the newspaper, and headed into the living room. Mom got me a few pillows and tucked some blankets around me on the couch.

"Honey, are you okay?" she asked, brushing the hair out of my eyes.

I nodded. I felt all right actually, just a little battered. "I'll be fine, Mom," I reassured her.

"I know you will," she said, standing up. "Just like your father. You've got a hard head — doesn't crack easily."

She stood there for a minute, staring down at me. For a second, it seemed as if she wanted to say something more, but then she just asked me what I wanted for breakfast.

After she left, I eagerly went back to the newspaper to find out more details about the game. Michel had scored the winning goal with seven seconds remaining in the third period. The paper said that Scottie had been sent to the penalty box just after I left, giving the Mongols a power play situation. That happens when someone gets sent to the penalty box on one team, because that team can't put in a substitute — it just loses a player. So the other team has a definite advantage. It has more players on the ice. But the Mongols couldn't capitalize, because Michel was playing like a pro. He held them off until Scottie got back in with ten seconds left and, in fact, assisted on Michel's goal. I was sorry that I had missed the game. The end sounded really exciting.

Emily came downstairs a little later and had breakfast with me in the living room. My mom never lets us eat in there, so I guess she was feeling really bad that I was hurt. Then Mom and Emily went to church. I couldn't believe I fell asleep again after all the hours I had slept the night before, but I guess I was still feeling a little shell-shocked.

Sabrina came home from church with Emily

and Mom. I must admit it felt pretty good to see my best friend.

"Katie!" Sabrina exclaimed as soon as she saw me. "You look terrible!"

"Thanks, Sabs," I said, trying to smile again.

"I didn't mean it like that, but ..." Sabs said, sitting down in one of the love seats across from the couch. "Do you think you'll have a scar?"

"The doctor said I'll probably get a scar, but they usually fade away in a few years," I explained quickly. "So tell me about the game. What happened after I left?"

"Well, first of all, the ice was totally covered with blood from where you fell," Sabs replied, scrunching up her face. "I though it was gross, but Randy said —"

"Sabs!" I exclaimed, laughing. "What about the game?" I asked her again.

"Oh, yeah," Sabs said quickly. "Right, the game."

"Right," I replied, pulling myself up from my reclining position on the couch. I really needed to sit up straight for this.

"Well, after you left," Sabs began, leaning forward, "Scottie got crazy. He was all over the ice, he was crashing into people every which way. I guess it was only a matter of time before the refs called him."

"Really?" I asked, surprised. I mean, I knew that Scottie had a bad temper and all, but he didn't have that many penalty minutes. At least, not compared to some of the other guys. He doesn't usually lose his head on the ice.

Sabs nodded. "And he got called for roughness when he practically tackled that guy who hit you," she said dramatically Sabs loves to be dramatic whenever she tells stories. She says it's good training for Broadway.

"You know what I think," Sabs went on. "I think that Scottie likes you and he was really upset when you hit the ice. I mean, he was the absolute first person to skate over to you when you fell. Then when the coach came over, Scottie started screaming for a doctor, and he looked totally worried. We didn't hear how you were doing until the end of the game, so Scottie was probably worried about you and made at that guy at the same time. Which is probably why he was acting so crazy during the rest of the third period."

I snorted. Well, at least, I tried to snort, but the sound that resulted was really more like a wheeze. "That's ridiculous, Sabs," I said, shaking my head. "You want to know what I think? I think Scottie hates me. He's been so mean to me since last week, and he's convinced that Michel is my boyfriend."

"What?" Sabs asked, with surprise. "Your boyfriend?"

"He even thinks Michel bought me my new skates," I went on, laughing. I didn't notice Sabrina's look of dismay at first. But when I stopped laughing, I could see clearly that her face had fallen. I had forgotten that she had a major crush on Michel. I hurried to reassure her. "Don't worry, Sabs," I said. "It's totally ridiculous. Michel and I are just friends. Really."

Sabs perked up immediately. "That's what I thought. I mean, you would have told me if you were more than just friends, right?"

I nodded. "So then what happened?" I asked, trying to get her back to the game.

"Well, then Michel started playing like Wayne Gretzky or something," Sabs went on, her face lighting up. "He was like a one-man team. So even though the Mongols had bigger players, they just couldn't take advantage of it."

"I am so glad that Michel moved here," I

said firmly.

"Me too," Sabs agreed.

"I mean, we would have lost without him," I went on, not really hearing her.

"Oh, yeah," Sabs said, nodding her head. "So then when Scottie came back in, there were only ten seconds left. Three seconds after that, he passed the puck back to Michel, who sent one of those hit shots flying toward the goal. It went right between the goalie's legs. I don't think he was expecting it."

"Sabs, that's a slap shot, not a hit shot," I corrected her with a giggle. "Anyway, I really wish I could have seen it," I continued, a little forlornly. The biggest game of the season, and I was getting sewn up in the locker room. It was totally unfair.

About ten minutes later, Allison and Randy showed up. Randy had brought a movie with her for us to watch — *Hide and Go Shriek*. Sabs wasn't too psyched, but she watched it any. I don't know why Sabs gets so scared. I mean, most horror movies are obviously fake. Mom was really nice and made us popcorn and stuff. She was definitely in a good mood. It didn't turn out to be such a bad day after all.

At about four-thirty, my friends went home. I suddenly remembered that the *nice* man my mother had met at the bank was supposed to be coming over for dinner. Well, at least my getting hurt hadn't been totally in vain. There was no way he could come now, not with me being injured and lying all over the couch. I settled back into the cushions, feeling satisfied for the first time all day.

"Oh, honey," my mom called from the kitchen. "Our company will be here in a little while. Why don't you go upstairs and get in bed. That way I can straighten up the living room."

"What?" I asked in surprise.

"Dinner will be on the table at six, Katie," my mom continued, poking her head into the living room. "I'd like it if you could sit at the table with us. But if you're not up to it, I'll help you get into bed."

I couldn't believe that *my* mother was still having this many over for dinner! Even worse, she didn't really care if I had dinner with them or not. If I didn't feel up to it, I could just go to bed. What kind of mother was this!

"Honey," Mom said, coming over and sitting on the edge of the sofa by my feet. "I'll understand if you don't feel like joining us for dinner. But I'd like it if you could try. I really want you to meet him."

I have to admit that she looked great. She was wearing another new dress. This one was black with little pearl buttons all the way up the back. I think it was silk. Anyway, she looked terrific, especially with her new hairdo. And she was sort of glowing, as if she was really happy about something. I decided that no matter how bad I felt, I couldn't let her down. Not when she looked so pleased. It wouldn't be fair.

"Okay, Mom," I replied, a bit reluctantly. "I'll go clean up and see what I can find to put on."

"I'm sure regular clothes would be uncomfortable," Mom said thoughtfully. "How about the beautiful green robe that Grandma gave you? You know, the one with the quilted top."

I nodded my agreement, and my mom hugged me. I made my way upstairs. Then I had another shock. Emily was waiting for me in the bathroom. She had already filled the tub with bubble bath for me.

"Hey, Katie," she said. "I hope you don't mind the bubbles."

"This is great, Emily! Thank you," I replied. And it really was great. Sometimes my sister totally surprises me.

"Don't worry about it, sis," she said, standing up and walking to the door. She paused and turned to face me. "You know, Katie," she began, hesitantly, "I know that I never really supported this hockey thing, but ... well, I just wanted to say that you were incredible yesterday. Dad would have been proud." And then she walked out, shutting the door behind her.

As I lay in the hot tub, my first thought was to wonder why I had not had a bath earlier. My muscles were already starting to feel better. I thought about what Emily had said. Dad would have been proud of me. Somehow, that thought made all my aches and pains almost seem worth it.

Chapter Eight

I was on my way downstairs forty-five minutes later, when the doorbell rang. I knew for a fact that it was on a quarter to six. He was early.

"Katie, could you get that?" my mom called from the kitchen. I walked over to the door and took a deep breath. This was it. I turned the knob and opened the door. My mouth dropped open in surprise. Michel was standing on the doorstep!

"Allo, K. C.," he said, grinning at me. "How are you feeling?"

"I'm okay, Michel," I replied, more than little confused. "What are you doing here?"

"I was invited for dinner," he said, obviously waiting for me to motion him into the house.

"What are you talking about?" I asked, now totally confused. What in the world was going on? "My mom invited some man she met at the bank over for dinner. She never said anything about inviting you, too. I didn't know that she even knew you." I held the door open for Michel and then took his coat. I couldn't very well leave him standing out on the front steps in the cold.

"She doesn't really know me," Michel said, looking around. "She knows my father. You have a very nice house, by the way."

"Thank you," I replied automatically. "Your father!"

"You didn't know?" Michel asked, his smile fading a little.

"No, I didn't know," I hissed as my mother walked out of the kitchen. "How long have you known?"

"Michel!" Mom exclaimed happily. "How are you? Congratulations! You boys played a great game yesterday."

"*Merci*," he replied, shooting a glance at me. I was trying to freeze him out with an icy glare, but with my face so swollen, I could tell that it wasn't exactly working. "But K. C. played very well, too. I think we were all inspired to win it for her after she got hurt."

They tried to win it for me? I started to smile, but stopped myself just in time. Michel was probably just making that up because he knew that I was mad at him.

"She sure did play well," my mom agreed, stroking my hair. "Where's your father?"

Michel laughed. "He forgot to get flowers, so he dropped me off and ran to the store."

"He didn't have to do that," Mom said, giggling a little. Then she looked from my grumpy face to Michel's nervous one. "Why don't you kids have a seat in the living room? I have to check the roast," she continued.

Wordlessly, I walked into the living room and perched on the edge of the couch. Michel sat on a chair on the other side of the coffee table.

"I thought you knew," Michel began. "We met your mother when we got our mortgage. She was really helpful."

I couldn't believe this. My mother must have known that Michel was on the hockey team with me. So why hadn't she said anything to me about it?

"How is your face, K. C.?" Michel asked, after a long pause. "How many stitches did you get?"

"Eight," I answered shortly. "My face feels

fine."

"I am so happy that we won yesterday," Michel went on, obviously trying to ignore my bad mood. "You were really tough out there."

I nodded at his compliment just as the doorbell rang again.

"I'll get it!" Mom called before I could even get up. She practically flew to the door and then paused to straighten her hair in the mirror.

"Hi, Jean-Paul," I heard my mom say.

"You look *merveilleuse,* Eileen," a deep voice with a heavy French accent replied.

As he stepped into view, I tried to appraise Jean-Paul Beauvais objectively. I wondered what Michel's mother had looked like because his father looked exactly like an older version of Michel. Even if I saw Mr. Beauvais on the street without having met him, I would have known that he was related to Michel.

"Jean-Paul, this is my daughter Katie," my mom said, motioning toward me.

"It's very nice to meet you," I said politely.

"Katie, I have heard so much about you," Mr. Beauvais replied, stepping forward to take my hands. "I feel as if I know you already. Your mother talks so much about you and your sister.

And of course, Michel has told me all about you and your friends — especially the cute one, Sabrina. Right, Michel?"

Michel thought Sabs was cute? I shot a look at him. He blushed and then glared at his father. Sabs was going to die when she found out.

"I am sorry I missed your game yesterday," Mr. Beauvais continued. "I hear you played wonderfully."

"Thank you," I replied, looking at Michel again. Poor Michel. His first hockey game at a new school, and his father hadn't even been there to watch. Even though I was made at him, I felt bad about that.

"I hope I'll be there for the next game," Mr. Beauvais continued.

He hoped? These were the state playoffs we were talking about here. Mr. Beauvais dropped my hands as my sister walked into the room.

"And this must be Emily," he said, taking one of her hands and kissing it. "I have a feeling that your mother probably looked a lot like you when she was your age."

"Hello," Emily said in the same icily polite ton I had used. "It's very nice to meet you."

"I'd better check the roast," Mom said, turning to go into the kitchen.

"I'll help," I offered quickly. I didn't think I could just sit there calmly in the living room being polite to Michel and his father, who just so happened to be dating my mother. The whole situation made me very uncomfortable. I hadn't seen my mother acting like this for ages since … since … since my father died, I suddenly realized. What did that mean? I felt very mixed up about the entire thing, so mixed up that I didn't even have words to express my confusion. I sighed deeply.

"You know, Katie," my mom began as soon as the two of us were in the kitchen, "I didn't even know until yesterday that Jean-Paul's son was on your hockey team. That certainly makes things easier — that you're friends with Michel already."

Easier for what? Was she planning on marrying Mr. Beauvais?

"Oh, good, the roast's done," Mom said, turning off the oven. "Do you think you could spoon up the mashed potatoes?"

Ten minutes later, the five of us were sitting around the dining room table. I ended up sitting next to Emily and across from Michel.

Mom sat in her usual seat at one end of the table, and Mr. Beauvais sat at the other end — in Dad's old seat.

Mr. Beauvais sliced the meat and served all of us. It was pretty quiet while we all filled our plates.

"A toast!" Mr. Beauvais announced, raising his glass. "To the Campbell women. Thank you for giving us such a warm welcome to America."

We all sipped from our glasses. And then we started eating. It was a good thing that Mr. Beauvais and Mom talked a lot, because Emily, Michel, and I were all very quiet.

I just wanted the whole night to be over. My chin was throbbing, my cheekbone ached, and my lip was sore — to say nothing of all my muscles.

Finally, we finished dessert. Mr. Beauvais started saying something about getting home because Michel had school the next day. And before I knew it, the two of them were gone. I barely even remember saying good-bye to them.

I stumbled up to my room and undressed in the dark. I was feeling very out of it and so tired, I could barely hold my head up.

"Katie?" Emily asked, knocking on my door. "Can I come in?"

I just lay there nodding for a minute before it occurred to me that Emily couldn't see me. Luckily, she just pushed open the door and walked inside.

"I know you want to go to sleep, but I have to talk to you for a second," Emily began a little hesitantly. Then she walked over and sat down at the bottom of my bed, near my feet. "Why didn't you tell me you knew his son?"

"I didn't know," I replied, fighting to keep my eyes open.

"Oh," Emily said, and then she didn't say anything for a long time.

I was starting to doze off when she finally spoke again. "Did you like him?"

Feeling really groggy, I thought about it for a second. Yeah, I guessed that in spite of it all, I had to admit that I did like Mr. Beauvais. He was nice and funny — a lot like Michel. I looked over at Emily and nodded.

"Me too," Emily agreed. "What are we going to do now?"

"What do you mean?" I asked.

"Well, just because we like him doesn't mean that we want him seeing Mom," Emily said with a shake of her long blond hair, as if what she was saying was totally obvious.

"Oh," I said.

"I mean, he'll be the first person Mom's dated since ... Dad ..." Emily let her voice trail off. "Don't you think it's too soon?"

"Yeah," I replied, snuggling deeper into the covers. But Mom had looked so happy tonight. She was practically glowing by the time we were eating the cheesecake. And she had giggled a lot. She hadn't laughed so much since Dad died. I felt very mixed up. Part of me wanted her to be happy no matter what, but part of me felt as if she was betraying Dad's memory or something by dating another man. I sighed and turned over.

"Well, I'll let you get some sleep, Katie," Emily said, standing up. "Good night. Sleep well."

"Good night," I replied, barely hearing the door shut behind her. I was so tired, but I couldn't get Mom and Jean-Paul out of my mind. My mother was usually so in charge. She was kind of strict with me and Emily — but I knew that was because she loved us. Mom seemed kind of uncertain about Jean-Paul, though. It was weird, kind of like she was the daughter and Emily and I were her parents. But I decided right before I fell asleep that there was nothing Emily and I could do about Jean-Paul except wait and see what happened.

Chapter Nine

"Hey, Katie!" Sabs called as she walked up to our locker. "What are you doing here? I thought you'd stay home today."

I grabbed my math book and turned to face her. "Morning, Sabs," I replied, trying to talk without moving the muscles in my face too much. Actually, I was much more sore today than I had been the day before. "I couldn't lie around anymore. My mom really wanted me to stay home, but I would have been bored." That was only partly true. The real reason I hadn't stayed home was that then I wouldn't have to think about Mom and Jean-Paul, and Michel and Scottie. "Besides," I quickly told Sabrina, "I'm feeling much better."

"You don't look better," Sabs blurted out, then covered her mouth with her hand.

I giggled. "I know, my bruises are a lot darker," I continued before she had a chance to apologize. "But that means they're healing. And the swelling in my lip is going down."

"Your lip does look better," Sabs gushed, trying to make up for her last comment.

Suddenly Randy ran up behind Sabs. "Hey, Sabs," she said. "Listen, I . . ."

Sabs didn't say anything for a minute. She started making those strange faces again — the ones where she opens her eyes really wide and raises her eyebrows practically up to her scalp. Randy's voice trailed off.

"Look who's here," Sabs cut in loudly. "Katie came in today."

Randy glanced at me and then opened and shut her mouth a few times. What in the world was going on? I had enough to think about without this strange behavior from my friends.

"Katie!" Randy continued in a strangled voice. "What are you doing here today?"

"I felt better," I said simply. "And I wanted to come to school. Is there anything wrong with that?" What I really wanted to ask was *Why all the secrets lately?*

Slamming the locker shut and forgetting that Sabs had to get into it also, I added, "I'll see you guys later." I quickly turned around and walked down the hall. I mean, they didn't have to tell me what was going on, but I hate secrets. I remember when I hung out with Stacy and her crowd the year before. They had so many secrets. Secrets always make the person who doesn't know feel really bad. And with that group I was sometimes the person who was left in the dark. So I know exactly how it feels. I expected stuff like that from Stacy, but not from my friends. I was really hurt — especially now with my accident and my mom dating and everything. I was no in the most coping mood.

"Wow! What's with her?" I heard Randy ask Sabs as I marched away. I don't know how I got through the rest of the day. I was groggy and upset all at the same time. No one could believe that I had come to school in the first place. Randy, Al, and Sabs tried to be nice to me, but I could tell that something was up that they weren't telling me about. At lunch they stopped arguing about something as soon as I sat down. That only made me more upset. I don't think I said two words the rest of the period.

Finally it was time for hockey practice. Actually, we were just having a team meeting because the coach was giving us a day off after the game.

"K.C.!" Flip called to me as soon as I walked into the rink. I was a few minutes late because I had waited until I was sure that Sabs had gotten her stuff out of our locker. I didn't want to feel left out of something again. "Come sit over here!" he continued, indicating the space next to him on the bench.

I walked over and sat down. "How are you feeling?" Brian asked from the other side of Flip. "We really missed you at the end of the game!"

"I'm much better," I replied, trying not to look at Michel, who was sitting next to Brian. He managed to catch my eye anyway and smiled at me. I glared back. "I'm sorry I wasn't able to see you guys win," I continued, turning back to Brian and Flip. "I hear it was really exciting."

"It sure was!" Flip exclaimed. "Michel was awesome!"

"Really!" Brian agreed. "And you missed the original iceman, Scottie Silver, totally losing control!"

I had almost forgotten about Scottie with all this other stuff going on. I glanced over at him, but he was staring straight ahead at the ice in front of us.

"So, how many stitches did you get?" Flip asked, unsnapping the front of his hockey jacket.

"Eight," I replied as I watched the coach make his way across the ice. Usually I love to watch him walk across the ice because he has kind of a big stomach, and he has this funny way of sliding along in his sneakers. I always think he's going to tip over. But I wasn't in a laughing mood just then.

"All right, team!" Coach Budd called out as he stopped in front of us. "I just wanted to congratulate you all on a good win."

The team clapped and cheered. By the time we had quieted down, the coach was looking a little more grim.

"There were, however, a few things I wouldn't want to repeat at the playoffs," he continued, looking right at Scottie. "For instance, what were you thinking, Silver, when you went on that completely unprofessional rampage?"

Scottie didn't say a thing. He just kept staring out at the empty ice.

"Well?" Coach Budd asked impatiently. "You're not the type to lose your head out there? What was going on?"

Scottie still didn't answer.

"Excusez-moi," Michel suddenly cut in. "I mean, excuse me, but I think we were all a little upset about what happened to K. C.."

"Ah, Campbell," Coach Budd said, looking at me for the first time. "How are you doing? You're definitely a hockey player now. How many stitches?"

"Eight," I replied softly, feeling almost proud.

The coach nodded and smiled slightly. "Well?" he asked, turning toward Scottie again. "Did your ... er ... behavior have something to do with what happened to Campbell?"

But Scottie was too busy glaring at Michel to see the coach. If looks could kill, Michel would have been a corpse right then.

"No, she had absolutely nothing to do with it," Scottie retorted through clenched teeth, turning back toward the ice.

"Whatever it was," Coach Budd said, giving up, "make sure it doesn't happen again. We can't afford to give anyone a power play situation like that again. If it wasn't for Beauvais ..."

Scottie snapped his head toward Michel again. "Yeah, right," Scottie muttered under his breath.

"Whoa," Flip whispered. "What is up with the iceman? He should be thankful that Michel is on our team."

I agreed. As the coach went on about our upcoming game, my mind wandered. I couldn't wait to get home and go to sleep. Even though I had told everyone that I was feeling much better, the truth was that I was still pretty whipped. I felt as if everyone was acting weird — Scottie, my friends, Michel — everybody.

Chapter Ten

Michel calls Sabrina.

MICHEL: *Bonjour.* May I speak to Sabrina, please?

SAM: Just a sec. Hey, is this Michel?

MICHEL: Oui.

SAM: Great goal on Saturday, dude. You played like Gretzky or something.

MICHEL: *Merci.* But it was more than just me. Bradley has a really good team. K. C. and Scottie are both very good players.

SAM: I know. But you were incredible! Anyway, let me get Blabs, I mean Sabs.

MICHEL: *Merci.*

SABS: Michel?

MICHEL: Sabrina, allo.

SABS: What are you calling me for? I mean … uh … Hello, Michel.

MICHEL: Allo, Sabrina. How are you?

SABS: Okay. What can I do for you?

MICHEL: Well, I was wondering if ... I mean, I know you are K. C.'s best friend . . . .

SABS: Right.

MICHEL: Well, I was wondering if you knew what was bothering her this week. She's been acting very strange since Monday, and ...

SABS: I really don't know. Listen, if you really like Katie, you should just call her yourself, okay?

MICHEL: Like K. C.?

SABS: I can understand it, Michel. I mean, she's really a great person and all. She is my best friend. And she's a great hockey player.

MICHEL: I don't like K. C.. I mean, I do like K. C., but not that way.

SABS: You don't? Really?

MICHEL: *(laughing)* Really.

SABS: That's great! I mean . . . uh . . . I mean . . .

MICHEL: I know what you mean. About K.
           C., though. She hasn't said two
           words to me since Sunday night.

SABS: What happened Sunday night?

MICHEL: My father and I went over to her
           house for dinner.

SABS: You did? Why?

MICHEL: Well, my dad is sort of seeing her
           mother.

SABS: WHAT?! I don't believe it! I can't
           believe she didn't tell me about
           that. Why didn't she tell me? She
           tells me everything. That's why
           she isn't talking to you, right?

MICHEL: But I don't understand it. I
           thought she'd be happy. I think
           my dad really likes Mrs.
           Campbell, and I think it would be
           good if K. C. and I were friends. I
           mean, I thought we were. Mostly, I
           hate it when my dad dates a
           woman who has kids because usu-
           ally I hate the kids. But I like K. C.
           And I *really* like her friends.Could
           you let me know if she says any-
           thing to you?

104

SABS: Sure, I'll let you know. No prob-
            lem. I can't believe your father is
            dating Mrs. Campbell. Wow!

MICHEL: By the way, Sabs, are you coming
            to the playoffs? I certainly hope
            you'll be there.

SABS: You do? I wouldn't miss them for
            the world.

MICHEL: *Bon.* Good. I've got to go now. I'll
            see you tomorrow in school, okay,
            Sabrina?

SABS: Okay.

MICHEL: *Merci.* Thanks for everything,
            Sabrina.

SABS: Don't mention it.

MICHEL: *Au revoir.* Good night.

SABS: Our river. I mean, good-bye.

Sabs calls Allison.

SABS: Al, this is Sabs. What's up?

ALLISON: Hello, Sabrina. How are you
            doing?

SABS: Fine, fine. Listen, I was just won-
            dering if you knew what was
            bothering Katie. I just talked to
            Michel, and he said she hasn't

been talking to him at all this
whole week.

ALLISON: Really? And he didn't know why?

SABS: Well, he said that his father and
Katie's mother are dating. And he
said his father really likes Mrs.
Campbell. I wonder if they'll get
married. But anyway, I knew
something was bothering Katie.
Why didn't she talk to us about it?
I mean, we're her best friends. I'm
really upset about this, Al.

ALLISON: Katie probably is, too. Sabs, I'm
sure that she wanted to tell us
about it, but she didn't know how.
It's probably hard for Katie to see
her mother is dating. After all, her
mother hasn't been out on a date
since her father died.

SABS: That's true. But why didn't Katie
tell me?

ALLISON: You know Katie likes to work her
problems out before she talks
about them. I wouldn't worry
about it, Sabs. She'll tell us when
she's ready.

SABS: Do you think so?

ALLISON: Definitely. So, did Michel say any-
            thing else?

SABS: What do you mean?

ALLISON: About liking you?

SABS: ALLISON!

ALLISON: Well, did he?

SABS: He did say something about liking
            Katie's friends, a lot.

ALLISON: I knew it.

Sabs giggles.

SABS: How do you always know these
            things?

ALLISON: I just get certain feelings about
            affairs of the heart. Are you going
            to call Katie?

SABS: I think I'd better.

ALLISON: I think you should, too. Let me
            know what happens, okay?

SABS: Okay. I'll see you at school.

ALLISON: Good night.

SABS: Bye.

Allison calls Randy.

RANDY: Yo!

ALLISON: Hi, it's Allison.

RANDY: Al! What's shaking?

ALLISON: I just talked to Sabrina. She's really
           worried about Katie.

RANDY: Why?

ALLISON: Well, Michel called her and it
           seems that his father is dating Mrs.
           Campbell.

RANDY: Whoa!

ALLISON: Exactly. And Katie hasn't been
           talking to Michel all week. Sabs is
           upset because Katie hasn't said
           anything to us about it.

RANDY: Well, Sabs and Katie are pretty
           close. I can understand Sabs being
           upset, but I'd probably freak if M
           started dating now. I mean, it's
           bad enough Dad's going out with
           someone now, but if M decided to
           date, I would definitely flip.

ALLISON: I know. Katie is probably not tak-
           ing her mom's dating very well.
           That's probably why she hasn't
           said anything. Sabs thinks that Mr.
           Beauvais is pretty serious. She
           even thought they might get mar-
           ried.

RANDY: Married? Isn't that rushing things a bit?

ALLISON: Well, you know Sabs.

RANDY: So, is Sabs calling Katie now?

ALLISON: Yes. And she said she'll let us know what happens tomorrow in school. Oh, and I was right about Michel and Sabs.

RANDY: You usually are. I think Katie will feel a lot better after Saturday, anyway.

ALLISON: I think you're right.

RANDY: Nothing like a surprise. Hey, listen, I've got to get a move on. M's working on a portrait series for a show coming up — and guess who's the subject.

ALLISON: Good luck. I'll see you tomorrow. Good night.

RANDY: *Ciao.*

Sabs calls Katie.

SABS: Hi, is Katie there?

KATIE: Hi, Sabs.

SABS: What's up? Listen, how are you feeling now? Does it still hurt to move around?

KATIE: Yeah, a little bit, but at least it's healing.

SABS: Well, I just called to see what"s going on. I waited for you by our locker after school, but I guess I must have missed you.

KATIE: Well, the team had a meeting. Then I felt really tired and I wanted to get home right away.

SABS: Well, I just want you to know that any time you want to talk to me, just call. Day or night, it doesn't matter. After all, we are *best* best friends, and you should know that you can count on me! So, talk to me, Katie. What's going on? How's your mom — and Emily, of course?

KATIE: Really, Sabs, everything's fine.

There's a long pause.

SABS: Hey, well, I talked to Michel. And guess what? He likes me! You were right. I'm so excited! He is so cute, and I love his accent. He sounds so ... so ... so French. It's

	so romantic. He told me that he likes your friends a lot. Al said he definitely meant me. I can't believe it. Can you believe it? Katie? Are you there?
KATIE:	I'm still here, Sabs. That's great. See, I told you so. Listen, Sabs, I really have a lot of homework to do. Can I talk to you tomorrow?
SABS:	Uh ... sure ... I guess so. Are you okay, Katie? Remember, you can call to talk anytime.
KATIE:	I'll remember, Sabs, and don't worry about it, okay? I'm fine.
SABS:	Sure. You know you can talk to me about anything, don't you?
KATIE:	Thanks, Sabs. But I really have to get some work done before bed. I'll see you tomorrow. Bye.
SABS:	Bye.

Chapter Eleven

I can't believe it. My mother forgot my birthday! Well, she didn't exactly *forget* my birthday — after all, I did get new skates. And she did say Happy Birthday when I came downstairs for breakfast. But that's it? We usually have plans, and she tells me to be home early because my grandparents are coming over, or stuff like that. But just Happy Birthday! What is happening to everybody?

Anyway, I couldn't stand hanging around the house any longer. So I went to Elm Park. It felt good to get some exercise and fresh air. And for a saturday, the pond was surprisingly empty. Thank goodness it was finally Saturday. The whole week had been too weird.

At least Michel wasn't skating at Elm Park. I really didn't think I could handle seeing him just then. All week, he had kept trying to talk to me. And I had kept ignoring him. I'm sure he felt the way I did when I tried to talk to Scottie on Wednesday after practice. He told me he was in a rush and practically ran off. I have no idea what I could have done to make him so mad.

I started skating around, trying not to think about anything. At about twelve o'clock, Allison suddenly showed up at the pond.

"Katie!" she called from the bench at the side.

I stopped short in surprise.

"Your mom said I could probably find you here," she went on as I got closer.

I skated in and sat down on the bench next to her.

"What's up, Al?" I asked in a soft voice. My legs were kind of tired, so I started unlacing my skates.

"I was just worried about you, Katie," Al replied, giving me this long look that seemed to go right through me.

"Well, you shouldn't be," I said quickly.

"Come on, Katie," she went on, pulling her green knit hat down farther over her dark brown hair. "We're your friends. Michel told us about Sunday night."

"He did?" I retorted angrily. "He had no right!"

"He was worried about you," Al replied gently. "He's your friend, too."

I didn't say anything — just stared stonily at the pond. "I know you're upset that your mother is dating Michel's father, Katie," Al continued. "I can imagine how you feel."

"No you can't!" I retorted. No one could possibly understand how I felt.

"Well, Randy can," Al went on. "She said she'd freak out!"

Hanging my head, I realized that Al was right. Randy could understand how I felt. Probably Al and Sabs could, too. They all know how much I miss my dad.

"Let me ask you something, Katie," Allison continued. "Don't get mad. But wouldn't your father have wanted your mother to do whatever she needed to do to be happy?"

Whatever question I expected, that wasn't it. "Of course he would have!" I exclaimed. "I do, too. But it seems so soon for her to be dating someone seriously."

"It's been three years, Katie," Al replied, putting her hand on my shoulder. "When is it not going to be too soon?"

Al stood up and started walking across the ice. I watched her, thinking that she was much better at keeping her balance than Coach Budd. Allison has this way of saying things that make you think. She knew without my saying a word that I needed to be alone for a few minutes to think about what she had just said.

After I unlaced my skates, I put my boots back on. I had to admit that Al had a point. My dad definitely would have wanted my mom to do whatever she had to do to make her happy. And three years was a long time. Just because she was dating someone didn't mean she was going to forget Dad. And even if she married Mr. Beauvais, I knew that she would still love my father.

"Are you okay, Katie?" Allison said suddenly, breaking into my thoughts. "Are you ready to go back to your house?"

I nodded slowly. Talking to Allison had made me feel much better about Mom and Mr. Beauvais. But it didn't really help with the other stuff that was bothering me — like the fact that my friends still had some kind of secret they weren't telling me about. But I didn't feel up to asking Al about it. They obviously didn't want to tell me about whatever it was. And I wasn't about to lower my pride and ask.

On the way home, I also realized that Allison had also forgotten my birthday. I couldn't believe it. I guess my friends and everybody else were so worried about my emotional state and my accident that it must have completely slipped their minds. But I still felt kind of depressed. I mean, here I was finally thirteen years old and a teenager, and no one cared.

My mom's car wasn't even in the driveway when we got back. Dejectedly I opened the front door and slowly stepped inside. Allison walked in right behind me.

"SURPRISE!!" all these voices yelled at once.

Startled, I took a step back. It seemed as if a hundred people were jammed into my living room.

"Happy Birthday, honey," Mom said, coming forward to give me a hug.

I couldn't believe it. I felt like crying. They hadn't forgotten my birthday after all.

"Thanks, Mom," I said, blinking furiously.

"It was all of your friends' idea," Mom

replied, smiling.

Sabs, Allison, and Randy just stood there, grinning.

"So that's what you guys were up to!" I exclaimed, suddenly realizing what their big secret had been. They hadn't been leaving me out of anything — they had been doing something that was all for me! "You guys are great!"

"You're surprised?" Sabs asked. "I was so afraid I was going to slip and spill the beans."

"I'm shocked," I replied honestly and then turned to look at the crowd of people in the living room. Everyone was there — all the guys on the hockey team — even Coach Budd!

Flip handed me a box as I walked farther into the living room. I tore off the wrapping paper. Inside was my very own orange-and-black hockey jacket with "K.C." embroidered on the front. I couldn't help it then — I started to cry.

"Thanks, guys," I said. "This is great. You guys are great!" Then I hugged them all, even Coach Budd.

I put my jacket on and went to show everyone.

"Here, K. C.," Michel suddenly said, walking up to me. "My father and I got you something."

He handed me a long, skinny package that I
knew could only be one thing — a new hockey
stick.

"I hope it brings you luck in the playoffs,"
Mr. Beauvais added, walking up to stand next
to Mom.

On an impulse, I leaned forward and kissed
him on the cheek. "Thanks, Mr. Beauvais," I
replied, looking at my mom's beaming face. Mr.
Beauvais put his arm around Mom. Then I
kissed Michel's cheek, too. "Thanks, Michel. I'm
sorry I've been so mean this week."

"*Ne rien.* It's nothing, K. C.," he said, blushing. "Listen, I'm going to go get some punch.
Do you want some, Sabrina?" Sabrina just happened to be standing next to Michel. I gave her
a big smile.

Sabs nodded as Michel ran off toward the
kitchen.

"He likes you, Sabs," I teased her. She giggled.

"Look, Katie," Allison suddenly said. "Here
comes Scottie. I think he want to talk to you."

Scottie? Scottie was here. "I thought he

hated me," I murmured.

"Just the opposite, I think," Al murmured back as my three turned and followed Michel into the kitchen.

"Happy Birthday, Katie," Scottie said, walking up to me.

"Thanks, Scottie," I replied. I still couldn't believe he was in my house, and talking to me no less, after the way he'd been purposely ignoring me all week.

"Listen … uh … Katie …" he stuttered. Then he kind of walked us into another part of the room that wasn't so crowded.

"So, Katie …" Scottie cleared his throat and said my name again.

"Yes," I prompted.

"Well, I just wanted to apologize," he mumbled, looking at the floor. "I know I acted sort of like a jerk. I mean, I wasn't very nice to you. I thought that you liked Beauvais. Then Sabs told me that your mom had bought you those skates and that Michel liked her. I guess I was just jealous."

Jealous? Scottie Silver was jealous because he thought another boy liked me?

"Then when you got hurt in the game … I

guess Michel was right," he continued, finally looking up at me. "I was kind of worried about you. I lost my head."

"Why?" I asked.

"Well, that's the reason I stopped asking you to go out," Scottie explained. I must have looked confused, because he continued. "Well, see, I've liked you from when you first tried out for the team. But I knew that if we went out, I'd be way too distracted on the ice. You know, because I'd be worried that you'd get hurt or something. And that would hurt the team. But then after you did get hurt, I realized that I was distracted anyway, because I still like you."

"You do?" I asked softly, not trusting my voice.

"Yeah," he admitted, touching the bandage on my chin. "Does this still hurt?"

"Nope," I answered, not taking my eyes from his. "In fact, I get the stitches out on Monday."

"Really?" Scottie asked, not taking his hand away from my face. "That's great." Then he leaned forward and gave me a quick kiss before I could even react. "Uh ... do you think you'd like to go to the movies with me sometime soon?"

"Sure, great," I replied, happily. I couldn't stop smiling.

Titles in the GIRL TALK series

1 WELCOME TO JUNIOR HIGH!
Introducing the Girl Talk characters, Sabrina Wells, Katie Campbell, Randy Zak, and Allison Cloud. When our four heroines meet and have to plan the first junior high dance of the year, the results are hilarious.

2 FACE-OFF!
Katie Campbell is just plain fed up with being "perfect." But when she decides to join the boys' ice hockey team, she gets more than she bargained for.

3 THE NEW YOU
Allison Cloud is down in the dumps, and her friends decide she needs a makeover, just in time for a real live magazine shoot!

4 REBEL, REBEL
Randy Zak is acting even stranger than usual — could a visit from her cute friend from New York have something to do with it?

5 IT'S ALL IN THE STARS
Sabrina Wells's twin brother, Sam, enlists the aid of the class nerd, Winslow, to play a practical joke on her. The problem is, Winslow takes it seriously!

6 THE GHOST OF EAGLE MOUNTAIN
The girls go camping, only to discover that they're sleeping on the very spot where the Ghost of Eagle Mountain wanders!

☆7 ODD COUPLE

When a school project pairs goody-two-shoes, Mark Wright, with super-hip Randy Zak as "parents" of an egg, Randy and Mark find out that they actually have something in common.

☆8 STEALING THE SHOW

Sabrina sets out to prove that she's perfect for the lead role in the school production of *Grease*, only to land herself in one crazy mix-up after another.

☆9 MIXED FEELINGS

Katie Campbell doesn't know whether to laugh or cry when Stacy the Great's best friend Laurel Spencer is chosen as her skating partner for the Winter Carnival.

☆10 FALLING IN LIKE

Allison's not happy about having to tutor seventh-grade troublemaker Billy Dixon. But when they discover a key to his problems, Allison finds out that you can't always judge a book by its cover.

☆11 MIXED FEELINGS

A gorgeous Canadian boy moves to Acorn Falls and life turns pretty interesting for Katie Campbell — especially when Sabrina likes the new boy and he likes Katie!

☆12 DRUMMER GIRL

It's time for the annual 'Battle of the Bands'. Randy decides to start her own all-girl band after she overhears the guys in Acorn Falls say that girls can't play rock 'n' roll!

LOOK FOR THE GIRL TALK SERIES!
COMING SOON TO A STORE NEAR YOU!

TALK BACK!

TELL US WHAT YOU THINK ABOUT GIRL TALK

Name _____

Address _____

City _____ State _____ Zip _____

Birthday: Day _____ Mo _____ Year _____

Telephone Number (____) _____

1) On a scale of 1 (The Pits) to 5 (The Max), how would you rate Girl Talk?   Circle One:

            1   2   3   4   5

2) What do you like most about Girl Talk?

___Characters___Situations___Telephone Talk

Other _____

3) Who is your favorite character?   Circle One:

    Sabrina   Katie   Randy

    Allison   Stacy   Other

4) Who is your least favorite character?

_____

5) What do you want to read about in Girl Talk?

_____

_____

Send completed form to :
Western Publishing Company, Inc.
1220 Mound Avenue Mail Station #85
Racine, Wisconsin 53404